THE
AMARISIAN
PROPHECIES

The Reckoning

ZOE NAUMAN

For Mum and Dad, who always said, since I was little "I know you have a book in you."
For my husband Grant, who has been unwavering in his support, love, and encouragement.
And for the Big Man upstairs, who gave me the inspiration to write this story.

The phone alarm pierced Nadia's slumber as she was pulled from her dreams and sharply into the reality of her bedroom. Opening one eye, she realized she had burrowed herself into her duvet. Sighing, Nadia pulled herself out of her bed and sat up. Running her hands through her shoulder-length brown hair, which looked like a bird's nest thanks to her tossing and turning through the night, Nadia absent-mindedly scratched her wrist. Her jagged birthmark had been itching all night.

Nadia stood up and padded over to the window. She drew back the curtains of her sixth-floor apartment and gazed at the London skyline which stood out sharply against the watery winter morning light. Looking out over the area between her apartment and the car park with its dark grey cement walls covered in graffiti, directly in front of her, on the other side of the block, was another long balcony with doors covered in iron bars like gawking eyes staring at her intently. On the far stairwell at the end of the walkway, she noticed a group of older teenage boys deep in conversation and clearly doing some kind of deal. Then the morning silence was pierced with the sound of a police siren.

They must be doing another raid, she thought.

The group of teens scattered on hearing the noise, running along the walkways and disappearing from view into dark and sinister corners. Gazing down into the car park below, Nadia saw movement under a dirty blanket, a shape huddled in the shell of a burnt-out car. She made a mental note to herself to take Fred a slice of toast. The rusted frame of the Audi glistened with frost, a clear indication he would have felt very cold during the night. Nadia sighed to herself and thought again of how determined she was to escape this rundown council estate where she lived. But first she had to get ready for school and get on with the business of getting through what would no doubt be another torturous day. She stumbled into the bathroom and gazed at herself in the mirror. Looking back at her was a thir-teen-year-old girl with hazel green eyes and a snub nose.

A memory of her dream flashed through her mind again, and she saw herself frowning.

It was always the same – a boy, about her age, maybe a bit older, covered in dirt and grime cowering from a gigantic, cloaked figure with a gnarled scaly hand outstretched with long hooked claws. She could not see the creature's face, but she felt such an evil presence it felt like it would suck her soul from her skin. Nadia would call out, but when she opened her mouth there was no sound. The boy would turn his eyes, a burnished yellow gold and full of fear, towards her. She always woke up before she saw what happened to the boy, and she always was left with a feeling like should be doing something but didn't know what or how.

"Why can't I have dreams about coping off with Harry Styles," she asked her reflection, then bent her head down towards the basin to clean her teeth and wash her face. After pulling on her uniform—a navy jumper and skirt, a pair of black tights, and a white shirt—she walked into the kitchen.

Nadia ate two slices of toast and gulped down a glass of orange juice, then went into the lounge with a bin bag and began to methodically pick up empty cans of lager, which were scattered and crushed into bent-out shapes around the settee. The ashtray was overflowing with cigarette butts and roaches, and the air was slightly murky with stale smoke. She opened the curtains and did her best to spruce up the cushions. Then Nadia picked up the debris, emptied the ashtrays, and deposited the trash bag into the bin. She then went into the other bedroom in the small flat to check on her father, to make sure he at least made it into bed. Nadia could make out the outline of his body under the sheets.

"Dad?" she whispered. Then she called a little louder, "Dad, I've left the Alka-Seltzer out for you, and some Berocca tablets. Should help take the edge off. I'll finish tidying up tonight when I've caught up with Mum."

There was a grunt from the lump that was her father's body under the covers. Nadia closed the door as quietly as she could, grabbed another slice of toast and a cup of tea from the kitchen, and picked up her school bag from the chair in the hall before heading out. Running down the stairwell to the car park below, she headed in the direction of the school. She paused by the burnt-out car wreck where Fred was stretching and rubbing sleep from his eyes. Nadia smiled and tucked a brown hair strand behind her ear.

"Hey Fred, thought you could do with this," she said while handing him a slice of toast and a cup of tea. "Sorry, we've run out of coffee. But this might help take the edge off the hunger."

Scratching his head through his woolly hat, Fred gave her a gappy smile and gratefully took the bread from her.

"Thanks, love. You always look after me. You're a good girl."

He took a slurp of the tea and regarded her thoughtfully.

"You know, you should walk along the river today instead of the main road if you have the time. I think I saw the two foxes, and it's still early enough to catch them."

Nadia smiled. "Thanks Fred, that would be ace, I've been

wanting to see them again after spotting them a few weeks ago." She turned and headed towards the back of the estate.

Nadia's phone beeped in her pocket as she walked along. She pulled it out excitedly hoping the message was from her mum. Her face fell as she read the text: *Soz love gotta work tonight. Can we make it next week? Mx.*

Nadia tried not to feel hurt. She hadn't seen her mother for four weeks. Every time she tried to organize something with Janey, she cancelled. The last time she had seen her mother, she had been showing off a particularly nasty black eye, courtesy of her new "boyfriend." Janey had attempted to cover it up with concealer, but Nadia could still see it, along with the track marks on her mother's arm. She knew it was up to her mum to get clean; there was nothing she could do to help her. Janey had been in and out of rehab as many times as Nadia had been in and out of foster homes.

Her father, Dave, was trying to hold their home together and had been doing well. Last night's drinking and stoner session, Nadia told herself, was a one off, a blip. She knew he was trying his best. But he struggled, and thanks to the estate with its network of easy access dealers, it was hard. *At least he wasn't injecting again.* Nadia gave an involuntary shudder at the thought. It was why she was determined to get herself in and out of school as quickly as she could and get their family out of this life and into another one. Texting her mum back she responded: *No problem. We can do it another night.*

Nadia arrived at the access road which separated the estate she lived in from the sugar factory which sat next to the water on the River Thames. The processing plant had not yet revved into life, pumping out its pungent fumes which permeated the air and hung around for hours in the atmosphere. The river, a dark grey-blue of ever-changing currents, glistened in the sunshine.

In the distance, she could see the Thames Barrier—the metal structure refracting and bending the light off its off-white domes. Beyond that was Greenwich Park, and the

Observatory. Nadia loved to go up there when she could and take in the view of London from the top of the hill. She made her way to the barbed wire fence, which cut the back of the industrial estate off from the river. Finding the hole she had used so many times before, she slid her bag through and then clambered through the opening. Standing on the other side of the wire mesh, she took in a deep breath.

Nadia walked a few steps on a muddy path, and she was suddenly surrounded by trees with the river to her left. It was like she wasn't even in London if she chose to ignore the grey outlines of the buildings across the water. She hitched her bag on her shoulder and kept walking. As Nadia walked along the river bank the path meandered into thicker group of trees.

Every now and again she picked out the shape of a bent bicycle or a pile of rubbish.

Nadia chose to ignore it. She hated what she saw as the suffocating grime of London. She loved nature and loved taking this walk to school. She could hear the sound of the birds, and the rush hour traffic was a distant and very dull roar. If she imagined hard enough she could pretend it wasn't cars at all but the sound of sea. It helped her feel like she had escaped her life, like she could be a different person. She longed to be able to move her whole family away from the city and into the countryside, but she had to figure out a way to do it. Suddenly into her line of sight moved a flash of colour. It zipped into and out of her vision, a streak of fuchsia and turquoise.

What was that? she thought.

She stopped. She figured it was a bird and wanted to get a better look at it. Nadia's breathing sounded so loud in her own ears, she wondered if the creature could hear it. Then the flash of colour was back. It darted backwards and forwards across the path, a blur of pink and blue. Nadia whipped her head backwards and forwards trying to follow it. She decided to stand perfectly still, and her patience was rewarded. A hummingbird sped past her again but then circled around and hovered about a foot away from Nadia's nose. She gasped in wonder as the tiny bird floated in the air in front of her, its wings beating so fast she could not even see them.

It seems to be looking at me, Nadia thought as she hardly dared breathe. The iridescent hummingbird did indeed stare at her, regarding Nadia quizzically. It then moved backwards and forwards, each time coming to a stop just in front of her nose.

"Do you want me to follow you?" she said to the bird and then caught herself. "I'm talking to a bird?!" she said out loud with a laugh as she shook her head.

The bird began to move frantically backwards and forwards. It did seem to want her to follow it.

"Ok," Nadia said, smiling in wonder. "I'll give this a go."

Feeling a bubble of excitement in her stomach, she began to walk in the direction the bird was moving, which took her off the pathway and into a thicket of trees. Nadia gasped as it came to a stop near what looked like an incredibly large, dark brown stone in the shape of an egg. Its surface was smooth and polished, almost like the surface of marble. The only mark on it was a jagged line, hewn into the rock running from the top to the bottom.

It seemed to belong with the trees around it but at the same time was completely out of place.

"Hmm this is weird; I've not seen this before. Do you know where this came from?" she asked the bird, then caught herself. "I'm talking to a bloody bird!!!! What am I doing?!" she said and shook her head again. The hummingbird hovered by the rock and then flew towards the jagged line.

It suddenly disappeared. "What?!" Nadia exclaimed, "where did you go?"

She moved around to get a better look, and as she changed positions, the jagged line split and opened, revealing an entrance into the rock.

This is weird, she thought, but decided events had been strange enough so far, so why not see what was inside. As she walked towards the split in the rock, it opened up even more, and she could see she could easily get in.

Nadia entered the stone and peered through the semi-darkness. Why had she never seen this before? She pulled her phone out of her pocket and tried to use the torch function. It wouldn't work. As she turned back to the entrance into the rock to get some light, she saw she had no signal. In fact, the face of her device had no time, no network, no power signal. Just a photo of herself and her mother smiling back at her.

Hmm, odd, Nadia thought.

Turning back to face the interior of the cave, she could make out strange drawings engraved on the stone. There was what looked like an elephant, but it had two sets of tusks. A woman with flaming red hair, an imperious haughty look on her face, and eyes as black as night. A winged man surrounded by a nimbus of light, carrying a sword. Something that looked like a unicorn, a twisted tower, two moons, and stars hewn into the rock. She could make out four comets and winged beings that looked like giant reptiles. As she peered more intently at the wall she noticed a boy with bright yellow eyes —the boy from her dream! He was in shackles.

"What the?" Nadia said out loud and traced his outline in the rock. She could also see the creature from her dream, wearing its cloak, the outstretched grasping gnarled claws coming straight towards her. Nadia involuntarily raised her hands to her throat. She turned and felt the ground change under her trainers. It didn't feel like dirt anymore but something smooth. Suddenly there was a groaning sound, and she felt the atmosphere shudder around her. A crisscross pattern like a spider web on the walls began to shimmer and glisten like liquid, lighting up with an ethereal glow. Nadia stared around her in wonder. She had never seen anything like it before. The walls pulsed with colours and mother of pearl ran through the rock. It felt like the stone was almost breathing, like it was alive. The ground started humming. She looked down and realized she was standing on a piece of metal in the shape of a hexagon. Its edges glowed red and pulsed with a beat, which she suddenly worked out was pretty much the same speed and her heart. Nadia looked around frantically, and when she turned to where the entrance was, there was now a solid wall.

She shouted. "Help, help, help me!" What was happening? This was too crazy.

The drawings on the walls were getting brighter and brighter as the liquid glowed and merged into a miasma of colours. Nadia had to squint her eyes as the light was blinding her. She gasped as she could make out the tips of waves and currents on the moving substance running through the lines and pictures on the walls. Nadia looked up and realized there was no ceiling. She could see the stars. Feeling sick and terrified she squeezed her eyes shut "This is a dream. This is a dream," she said to herself over and over like a mantra.

Then with a huge jolt Nadia was swept off her feet and was shooting up and up. Her face and skin stretched, her lungs felt as if they were in a vice, and her arms were pinned to her sides with the G-force. Nadia was shooting upwards at what seemed a thousand miles an hour into nothing. She opened one eye a sliver and before her was the hummingbird, beating its wings in slow motion. As Nadia gave a silent scream, she could have sworn she heard the bird say, "Hold on tight."

---

*A*fsana trudged along the dirt track precariously balancing a loaf of bread on her head. Her long plait swung as she picked her way through the stones and gravel. Dust covered her sandals and legs in a fine film of dirt. She desperately wanted to scratch her wrist but was trying to hold the loaf in place as she walked. The sun was slowly setting over the refugee camp where she and another thirty-five thousand people had set up a temporary home on the Turkish border with Syria.

She wound her way through the tent city—shacks made from wooden and metal poles, with just a piece of tarpaulin offering privacy for families of up to ten people who all slept where they could find space, even on the floor. The smell of cooking began to fill the air as nightfall approached. It was a mix of cooking food and petrol coming from makeshift stoves. With such a huge population in such a small area, there was always hustle and bustle, so much so that people never really slept. Which was just as well when your front door was a dirty sheet and body heat from your siblings was the closest you got to heating.

Afsana smiled and nodded as she passed her neighbours. She stopped by her father's stall. Kadim was busy hustling with an old man with a grey beard over a battered box of flour.

"Come on, you know how hard these are to come by. I cannot come down on the price."

The older man looked at him pleading. "I need it for my granddaughter. She gave birth a month ago and needs to keep her strength up to feed her baby. You know the rations we have just aren't enough."

Kadim's face was hard set, and he ran his hand backwards and forwards over his short dark hair.

"Ok, Ok, but you owe me one. Next time you get a job outside, I want a cut."

The older man smiled in relief. "You have my word, Kadim," he said. "You are a good man. Inshallah, you will be looked on kindly for this."

"Yes, yes, I know, and my riches will be in Heaven," Kadim smiled. "Now go and don't tell anyone or I will have everyone thinking they can get a discount."

As he held his hand out for the coins, he turned and saw Afsana standing in the lengthening shadows.

"My beautiful daughter! Ahh, the baker looked after you today! Did they give you payment as well?"

Afsana placed the wrapped loaf on the ground in its rags, reached inside the pocket on her khaki skirt, and fished out the nine Turkish Lira. "Yes father," she said. "I know it is not much—"

"My sweet girl," Kadim said as he smiled and gave his daughter's arm a squeeze.

"You toiled twelve hours for this, and extra bread is more than you know. We can enjoy a feast this evening and then have some to sell tomorrow. When your mother returns from her rounds at the clinic, she will get to work and make us a wonderful dinner! Now you have half an hour before you need to return to help her. I would make the most of it."

Afsana smiled, turned, and ran back down the dirt path.

She paused at a crossroads in the hotchpotch of multi-coloured tents, and absent-mindedly scratched her wrist.

The flour seems to have made me scratch today, she thought, looking down at the jagged mark outlined on her skin. Afsana began climbing up the rubble and dirt of the hill towards the top of the camp. The higher she climbed, the sparser the rows of tents got. It was harder to set up living accommodation higher up. The electricity frequently cut out, and the generators were old and hard to come by. She turned and took a breath, looking down across the seething humanity below her.

Suddenly into her head came a memory of people screaming and running, the noise of bombs, machine guns, and shouts. Afsana put her hands over her ears and squeezed her eyes shut. "Get out, get out," she said to herself, as she tried to erase the images which flashed through her mind. The memories vanished as soon as they had come, and she gave a sigh of relief.

Afsana opened her eyes and ran towards the perimeter fence. Looking left and right, she could see in the distance the armed guards patrolling the barbed wire, rifles poised under their arms ready to fire should anyone try to make a break for it.

Afsana came to a metal pole on the fence and knelt down. She removed two large white rocks. She looked both ways again and then pulled up the wire, wriggling through the gap.

Looking behind her to check no one could see, she ran up the last few feet of the hill.

Stretched out below Afsana were hills. and rocky terrain. In the distance lights from towns and villages flickered. The sun was hanging low in the sky, and the barren landscape reflected its golden orange light. She breathed slowly. With the camp behind her over the hill, she could imagine she wasn't a refugee, living in a house made from metal poles and sheets of plastic.

For a moment she thought about running away and never coming back. But she knew she couldn't. Her mother and father needed her. They needed her to bring bread and wages to help them save up to find freedom. As their daughter she knew she could be the key to them being given asylum. And only then could she realize her dream of being a nurse like her mother, but in a country where she could practice.

Afsana sighed and sat down on the rocks and hugged her knees. She knew she had about twenty minutes before the guards came to her part of the perimeter. And then the flood-lights would go on as dusk descended. Gazing at the terrain below her, she suddenly noticed a flash of colour.

A tiny bird whirred in front of her—and hovered.

"A hummingbird!" she gasped, "What are you doing here?" The bird flew backwards and then towards Afsana again, its iridescent wings a blur of colour.

"Hey little bird, where are you taking me?" She smiled and then got up and walked after it. The bird darted to the right. Afsana saw a huge pile of boulders, which she had never noticed before. She picked her way through the rocks and walked around to discover there was an opening just big enough for her to crawl in. The hummingbird darted inside. Afsana looked at the hole and looked at the fence. She had enough time to crawl in and check it out. Maybe there was a nest in there? She crouched and wriggled through the gap.

She gasped as she came through the boulders and looked up. Scrambling to her feet, she could feel empty space above her head. She appeared to be in a cave and above her head were tiny glimmers of light. "Almost like stars," Afsana said to herself, "but that's not possible. It must be in the rock." She realized her feet were bathed in a red glow, which was emitting from the floor.

Curious, she thought and bent down to touch the rock. It felt like it was heating up. Afsana, feeling mildly panicked, turned to crawl out the hole she had used to get into the boulders. It was gone. She looked around her wildly. What to do? Then she felt a rush of air like a strong gust of wind. It knocked her off her feet. She appeared to be sitting in a hexagon marking on the floor of the cave. The hummingbird suddenly appeared in front of her. "Get ready," a voice said.

Afsana looked at the bird and raised an eyebrow. "Was that you?" she muttered. It seemed to stare at her intently. Suddenly marks began to appear on the walls of the cave. They pulsed slowly with light. Afsana looked around her and swallowed. A noise seemed to reverberate in her head and a pressure built around her, which felt like it was about to fire her into the stratosphere.

---

*A*bsolon was tired. Bone weary, because at two hundred eons old, he really should have left this world and moved onto the next. But the Divine wasn't letting him go. Absolon had witnessed so much heartache, misery, and destruction sometimes it was hard for him to continue to believe.

But he carried on living because he knew the moment he had been born for, had lived his whole life for, was almost here.

The heavens and Yasha Prophecy had foretold the world of Amaris would break from the iron grip in which it had been held for 150 eons by the evil Queen Sathariel, and the planets and constellations were aligning. Slowly putting one foot in front of the other, and resting heavily on his twisted staff, Absolon made his way up the stone stairs to the top of the tower. Even in his exhausted state, he felt a fizz of excitement.

As he stepped out onto the stone parapet, the fierce wind lashed at his wizened body. His shock of white hair, whipped around as the rain quickly saturated each strand. Absolon pulled his long voluminous robe closer, trying to keep out the biting cold. As the storm clouds scudded across the night sky, the constellations embroidered in silver thread caught the moonlight and looked as if they were slowly spinning in space. Absolon's eyes were a dark stormy grey-black like the rain leaden sky. He clenched his jaw in anticipation, accentuating his angular bone structure which he disguised with a close-cut beard, as he braced himself against the elements. Around Absolon's collarbone and neck was a web of tattoos, which were just visible. His skin was inked with a series of unidentifiable symbols and patterns. On his hands, he wore several intricate rings. One was made from twisted branches. Another was inset with a piece of rock that glittered with minerals. A third looked as if the sea itself was broiling within its depths. Around his wrist was a wide band of leather, which was covered in tiny bird feathers. His adornments were more than just jewellry; they were symbols of his ability to command the power of Ruacha, the energy that ran through the universe itself, and every living thing on Amaris.

Offering up a word of thanks to the Divine for giving him the ability to read the heavens, he pushed against the pouring rain across the battlements of the tower.

Absolon stood for a moment, catching his breath, and cursed, "How I hate this tired old body and yearn for that which once was." The sky opened up above him, full of rage with the storm. "I need to see the stars," Absolon muttered and raised his arms to the heavens. He concentrated on gathering the power of Ruacha.

As one of the four divine interpreters on Amaris, Absolon was able to harness its energy. He began to feel the draw of the power within him; his body felt like it was humming with the vibration. His blood was pulsing with an effervescent warmth in his veins, and the sound of his own heart filled his ears with its steady beat. He was filled with a euphoria that welled up inside him like a swollen river that was about to burst its banks. Slowing his breath, he concentrated on siphoning just enough Ruacha, despite the desire to let himself be engulfed in its power. Around his neck hung a metal pendant, which was engraved with two hummingbirds, their beaks touching. It began to pulse with a crimson glow. The divine interpreter stood in the centre of the stone pulpit and slammed his staff down into the star-shaped hole carved in the floor slick with rain beneath his feet. The atmosphere around him shimmered, glistened, and warped, sparkling with hues of pale pink, quartz, and rose—a force field he had put in place to keep out the prying eyes of the dark forces.

As Absolon concentrated on the sky clearing above him, the storm clouds began to dissipate, and the rain slowed to a drizzle. The wind dropped to a cool breeze, and the shadowy outline of the forest and mountains emerged. The silhouette of a broken, ravaged city was inky black in the distance. Absolon gazed up at the now clear night sky from his vantage point on the Tower of Sikuli. It was one of four impenetrable fortresses which remained after the Battle of the Shattering, the war that had raged across Amaris before the world had fallen into the grip of the dark forces. The towers were each held by one of the divine interpreters. Three were shrouded with a protection blessing which meant all who entered were safe from Sathariel's Malevolents.

Breathing in deeply again, he shut his eyes and offered up words to the Divine, "Help me see the sign," he said. "Show me the hope which was promised in the Yasha Prophecy. I know the moment is nearly here. The constellations have foretold it. The signs have been there. Help me see."

Breathing out slowly Absolon opened his eyes. Looking to the heavens he stared intently up at the stars twinkling above him. And then . . . the breeze dropped. The air was still. The moon Pythas, milky white and the smaller of the two gigantic satellites which hung in the sky, passed across her larger sister, Agoras, which was angry red. As Amaris swung into perfect alignment in the heavens, Pythas blocked out the other moon's light completely. The landscape was covered in darkness as the planet passed through the eclipse. Absolon held his breath, daring not to believe. Then he saw it: four tiny glimmers in the darkness, brighter and more brilliant than the other twinkling lights in the sky, shooting across the heavens. Four comets blasting through the dense void. They were getting larger and larger and their light more and more intense.

Pythas passed over her sister, and the brilliant glimmers disappeared into the mass of twinkling lights in the heavens. Absolon smiled and slowly shook his head in amazement. Then a huge grin spread across his face, and he started laughing. His whole body felt like it was immersed in warmth as he shook with mirth. He laughed so hard and loud tears ran down his cheeks, and he bent double as his sides hurt and ached with the intensity of his guffaws. Nearly hoarse he straightened up and shouted with exaltation.

"They're coming! They're coming! THEY'RE COMING!"

2

Husam was dirty, tired, and hungry. His hunger was almost like a friend now, such was the gnawing pain in his gut, which never left him; it just ebbed and flowed like a continuous tide.

How long he had been in the Mines of the Malevolents, he did not know. Time had lost all meaning. In his darkest moments he still clung to the memories of open fields, playing with his mother by the river and feeling the warmth of the bright sunshine on his skin. Husam was too scared to open his eyes because he knew he would lose his memories and be jolted back into his horrendous reality.

"Get UP!" A snarling voice echoed down the carved stone corridor. Reluctantly Husam stretched and sat up. He rubbed sleep from his eyes, as did the other twenty boys packed into the room. All of them had skin smeared with dirt, matted hair, and patches of dry blood on their bodies from the frequent lashings they had to endure.

Husam reached for his leather jerkin, the only protection he and the others had from the shards of rock, which would often hit them as they dug in the dirt. He rolled his ankle around, which was tight from the shackles.

"Hey!" shouted the youngster who was chained to him.

"Watch it! When you do that, we all feel it." He pointed to his leg which was pulled at an odd angle where Husam had tried to give his own limbs some release.

"Sorry," he mumbled and scratched at his chaffed skin.

There was a thunderous roar and heavy footsteps. The little bit of light which came through the barred opening in the door was blocked out by one of the Legion soldiers. Its black eyes peered through the bars. There was the noise of a padlock being opened and a rusty chain being released. The soldier entered and blocked the doorway with its girth.

Looming above the cowering boys in the gloom, the creature gave a guttural snarl. Its face still had traces of humanity, but from its lower jaw were two yellowing tusks and lips which glistened with saliva. The Legion soldier's nose appeared to be more of a snout, and the creatures' huge bulk was muscular and covered in hair like a goat. It wore a breastplate, which was embossed with a serpent.

"Pay allegiance to our Queen Sathariel," the creature grunted; its face contorted as it twisted its mouth to speak in a human tongue.

The boys bowed their heads as one and muttered, "We are thankful that she allows us to walk this day and provides."

Husam mouthed the words but did not say them. Instead, he prayed to the Divine to keep the mining sergeant from seeing he hadn't spoken out loud. The last time he got caught, he spent forty days and nights in solitary confinement and twenty lashes on every one of them.

The youngsters formed a single-file line. Husam, who was at the front of the chain gang, raised his head but made sure to keep his eyes down and his hair covering them as much as possible. His neck was encased in an iron collar, and the Legion soldier clipped a ring through it which was attached to rope. Yanking Husam and the rest of the boys, they were all forced to fall into line and began their slow march down into the mines.

They walked in a line through the black stone corridors,

which were lit with flickering torches. There was a dull rhythmic thudding which reverberated through the tunnel and was slowly getting louder and louder. Husam shuffled along behind the Legion soldier.

Every day he prayed to the Divine to somehow be released from this hell which was his life. Husam scratched his wrist again and then made sure the marks on it were covered. His mother's face came into his mind, gazing at him, full of fear, worry, and kindness. The words she spoke the last time he saw her echoed in his mind: "We don't have much time Husam. They are coming to get you, along with all the young boys who are of age. Promise me you will stay strong, and do not give up. Do not forget the Divine is watching over you, however bad things may seem. You are the Chosen. You must always trust in that. Your mark is the sign of that. And your eyes, my beautiful boy, your eyes. Make sure they never see your eyes."

His mother had handed him a phial of green liquid and told him to drink. "This will help dull the colour of your eyes my beloved son," she had said. "But it will only last for so long. Pray to the Divine that the prophecy will be fulfilled before they discover who you really are."

Husam remembered his mother's gentle hands on his cheeks as she kissed his forehead. He gazed down at his wrist. The strange patterns on his skin were barely there now. They had been lightened with repeated packs of herbs by his mother when Queen Sathariel ordered the reaping. She was determined to find and kill the Chosen, by taking the firstborn of every family when they reached what had come to be known as the forbidden age. If she couldn't find the Chosen, she would make sure no boy was free. Now any boy who was of age was imprisoned in the Mines of the Malevolents. It was here that Husam was careful to keep the faded marking on his skin hidden; he knew the consequences if he didn't.

Husam was jolted back to reality as the rhythmic thudding got louder and louder. He and the rest of the boys were walking towards a fiery light which was slowly beginning to illuminate the walls with an intense red glow. The sergeant came to a stop and turned right. He pulled Husam's chain, forcing him to follow.

He squinted his eyes as they were pulled into an underground cavern that stretched up so high the ceiling disappeared into darkness. The hewn rock glistened in the glow of lava pits which plunged down into the core of the earth, filling the cavern with an intense heat. Long lines of youngsters, all as dirty and despondent as the boys with Husam, trudged their way down stone walkways cut into the huge walls towards the floor of the mine. Members of the Legion, all as grotesque as the creature who led him, stood at intervals on the path, armed with spears and bugles so they could communicate across the vast space. On the floor of the cavern, groups of youngsters were pushing carts of rubble towards the pits and hacking at the rock with sharp instruments. They were also suspended on platforms on the walls, picking away at the rock surface.

Husam recoiled as he looked up at the Malevolents, five in number, circling lazily as they flew slowly through the air. The Malevolents had hands like humans but were covered in reptilian skin with fingernails more akin to claws, and their arms were blood-red leathery wings. Their bodies were obscured by long, dark cloaks. Their faces were hidden in the dark recesses of their hoods. Their presence struck fear into the hearts of the children, like icy tendrils wrapping around their souls. They watched continuously, circling slowly.

Husam had never seen one of them land. But there were stories of what happened when one did. Of boys being struck dead by the touch of their flesh or looking on their face. But that was considered a better fate than those who got taken away. Those boys never returned, and no one knew where they went or what happened to them.

The Legion soldier pulled the collar around Husam's neck as they made their way onto the cavern floor. He then turned to a large stone basin full of mining tools and began handing them out. The boys filed over to one of the cliffs faces and climbed into a wooden cage, which the mining sergeants winched up to one of the platforms. Climbing out onto the ledge, they sat down precariously. Husam crossed his legs and began to slowly chip away at the rock.

The youngsters were there to find akatalite – a metal which was said to be indestructible. Incredibly rare, it was hard to find and ran in tiny fissures in the rock, which were so fine that it could only be detected in miniscule amounts. Anyone who possessed a weapon or protective armour made from it was, they said, impossible to kill. The Mine of the Malevolents was the last known place it existed on Amaris. And Sathariel was determined to have it all.

Husam blinked back tears while trying to stay strong. He had to believe his mother, to hold onto her words that he would somehow fulfil his destiny. He just couldn't work out how.

3

Divine interpreter Azvameth strode through the corridors of the Dark Fortress. His red cloak fanned out behind him as he walked with purpose towards the throne room. With skin as white as alabaster, its translucency gave him the appearance of being porcelain like. And it was stretched so tightly over his skull that every angle of his bone structure jutted through it.

Azvameth gripped in his hand a twisted staff so tightly that if he were a normal human being, he would have drawn blood. But this man had given up his humanity. He had turned his back on the Creator long ago. He had done a deal with Sathariel and embraced Ruach, the dark side of the power of the universe.

He reached the entrance to the throne room, where two of the Legion stood guard in front of towering doors. They lowered their spears to bar his way.

"Let me through!" Azvameth barked at them, sneering with disgust. The throne room was dark. The walls were carved out of the black rock, which glistened in the light cast from flames in a giant pit at the center of the vaulted space. Shadows licked up the walls in strange, contorted shapes, which looked like human bodies writhing and twisting in pain.

Standing near the pit was a being that appeared to be a woman. Her age was indeterminable. Not a wrinkle marked her skin. Her fiery red hair, shot through with gold, was twisted and piled intricately on top of her head in huge coils. Entwined into the tendrils was a black crown. In it was an emerald jewel which pulsed like a beating heart. This being had decided to assume the shape of a woman, for the woman is the seductress, the beauty, the intellect, the mother who can give life, and, if she wishes, take it away. She inhabited a body which made men weak at the knees, inspiring lust and misguided love –the kind for which men went to war for and women envied. Yet her beauty was cold and hard. Her eyes burned with an intensity as if the fires of hell were held within them.

This was Sathariel.

Her skin had an ethereal sheen, and it was so sheer in substance her veins could be seen within it. There appeared to be some kind life force coursing through her body, but it was not blood which sustained her. Sathariel's dress clung to every curve and plunged to her navel. She appeared to be deep in thought, staring out through a large hole at the far end of the room, which was hacked into the rock like and angry mouth.

A Legion soldier, who had stepped forward as the divine interpreter walked into the room.

"Mistress, Azvameth is here seeking audience."

Sathariel turned and rested her gaze on the soldier. He had sunk to one knee to make his announcement and looked at the floor. He dared not meet her eyes.

The soldier, like those who worked in the Mines of the Malevolents, had once been a man, but now, after pledging his allegiance to Sathariel, his features had twisted and distorted. His body was hulking and broad. The Legion wore a black breastplate which was embossed with a pitchfork surrounded by flames.

As Sathariel turned her dress rustled with a gentle sigh.

"He will no doubt tell us the time has come for the Reckoning. The army will have to be awakened."

Azvameth walked towards Sathariel and then lay down on the floor in front of her, his face pressed into the stone.

"Mistress will you permit me to stand in your presence? I have news as it is forewarned."

Sathariel gestured and said, "Stand and speak."

"Mistress, the stars have aligned. The comets appeared in the sky, and the time of the Reckoning is here. My spies are currently out looking for a sign of where they have landed on our world."

Sathariel narrowed her eyes. "How long before we know?" she hissed. "We must stop them coming together. If we can capture one of them before that happens and turn them, we can stop the prophecy. "They must not find the Chosen."

"My queen, they are due to come back to me by dawn," Azvameth said. "We are trying to find them before they make their way to the safety of one of the divine interpreters. Once they are within the confines of the Tower of Sikuli, we cannot reach them."

Sathariel turned towards the cavity in the rock. "Very well," she said. You do not serve me to give me answers that don't further our cause. This must be stopped. Or we will all suffer the consequences." She turned to the opening in the wall which began to swirl with mist and called, "Come forward!"

Suddenly, a dense fog obscured the nighttime landscape. Through the mist a shape began to appear, and a cloaked figure emerged into the room glided into the room as if walking on air. Eyes glowing like fire were where a face should have been.

The leader of the Malevolents got down on one knee, and his wings rustled underneath his cloak as he placed his gnarled reptilian hand on the floor.

"Mistress, I am here answering your summons. What is it you wish of me?"

Sathariel paced slowly as she addressed the Malevolent. "It seems despite our best efforts, the Yasha Prophecy is coming to pass," she said. "The Divine has found a means of trying to wrestle back control of this world. The Reckoning is upon us as foretold. The army must be assembled. Do we have enough akatalite?"

If death had a sound, it was the Malevolent's voice. Azvameth felt shivers down his spine and fear clutch at his heart as the creature spoke. "I will do what is necessary. Your will be done. Do we have your permission to gain strength from the prisoners?"

Sathariel gave a cold, cruel smile. "Of course," she answered. "The time has come; you need not ask. Take them, kill them, and do what is necessary to amass your strength. You have been caged for too long, you and the rest of your brothers."

She walked forward and placed her hand on the Malevolent's cloaked shoulder. "Your hunger shall be fulfilled," Sathariel said with a mirthless laugh.

The creature gave a sigh, which was filled with a despicable and insatiable longing. "Thank you, Mistress. We will not disappoint you when the time comes for us to be unleashed." He stood and vanished into the swirling mist.

Sathariel turned away from the cavity in the wall and dismissed Azvameth with a flick of her wrist.

"Leave me."

She turned her gaze back to the gaping maw in the rock. She looked out across the dark landscape and shut her eyes. "I did not assume this mortal body and sacrifice so much to lose control on this world," she said to herself. Looking up to the heavens she smiled cruelly. "Do you think I will let go so easily? Do you not think I know the pain it causes to see your people in pain and suffering? Do I not know what that suffering is?"

Sathariel's voice rose to a roar. "I will not be cast out again. The innocence of these children will not defeat me! Yasha, I know you are coming. And I WILL BE READY!"

<hr>

$\mathcal{N}$adia felt as if her skin were being sucked back into her own skeleton as the g-force pinned her to the side of the rock. Her brain was turning a thousand times an hour in her skull. She felt she was screaming so loud her vocal cords where about the shatter into a million pieces, but there was no sound. Then just as her body felt like it was about to split apart six ways—nothing.

Nadia was weightless, floating, not in herself. She slowly opened one eye and felt a surge of panic. She was indeed floating about ten feet off the floor. She drifted slowly up to the ceiling of the hollow rock and gently bobbed against it.

"Don't panic," she sternly told herself. She looked at her arm, and it seemed to move in slow motion, like she was swimming through treacle. *Is this what it's like being in space?* she mused to herself. She decided to try and somersault.

As she slowly turned 360 degrees, she burst out laughing. Coming to an upright position, she did a breaststroke manoeuvre and got into a position where she could hold onto a piece of rock. This all felt like it took a matter of minutes, but in reality, it was over in seconds. Then Nadia saw the hummingbird. He too was moving in slow motion. She could see every beat of his tiny wings as he flew into her line of sight.

"Brace yourself!" the bird said.

"Did you say that out loud?" Nadia asked.

Then in that instant, she heard a loud whistling. Nadia was glad she was holding onto the rock as the weightlessness was quickly replaced with a feeling of falling. Fast. Like an airplane crashing from the sky, the rock began to drop at what felt like a thousand miles an hour. Then with a huge shudder, they were still. Nadia fell to the floor with an unceremonious thud. She rubbed her neck and picked herself up.

The hummingbird whizzed into view. "Come on we have no time."

Nadia frowned. "What the? You *are* actually talking!"

"No time, no time!" the bird said as his wings zipped back and forth in a blur. "My name is Alar. We *have* to get to safety! Follow me!" The hummingbird flew straight at the rock face in front of Nadia. "Just walk through!" he frantically tweeted before disappearing.

Nadia looked at the rocky wall in front of her with fear and trepidation. Then it suddenly appeared to shimmer as if it were made of fluid.

"Ok, here goes nothing." Nadia braced herself, got into a starting running position, and hurled herself at the wall. Much to her surprise it was as if she had jumped into empty air and the next thing she realised, she was landing in a pile of leaves. Picking herself up off the floor she brushed herself off.

Nadia realized wherever she was, it was early dawn. And she appeared to be in a forest. Trees like the giant Redwoods she had seen in textbooks towered above her. Strange screeching and squawking sounds came from the trees. A mist swirled gently around her feet, and the ground was covered in dark green ferns and a carpet of dead leaves.

The hummingbird zipped into view.

"This way, this way," he commanded urgently and flew about twenty feet ahead of her.

"What's your name?" Nadia asked.

"Alar," the bird said. "You must follow me."

Nadia looked up at the sky and saw two moons pale and receding in the dawn light. "Well, this ain't Earth that's for sure!" she said out loud, giving a low whistle.

"You're not in Kansas anymore!" Following the little bird at a brisk trot, she began to have the feeling she was being watched. It wasn't in a bad way, more like she was being regarded with curiosity and expectation. Twice she thought she saw the leaves of the trees twitch from the corner of her eye. She never quite saw anything but was aware she definitely was not alone.

Nadia broke through the edge of the forest, and the ground opened out into a large clearing. There, in the middle of a field of swaying grass was a tall white building. A mass of turrets and spires rose into the sky like bleached twisted branches. The stonework looked as if it were a living breathing thing. Nadia could also see a thin rainbow hued shell reaching out in a perfect circle about a hundred feet from the base of the structure.

Alar whizzed backwards and forwards. "Nearly there," he said. "We have to get inside quick!"

Nadia turned and was shocked to see behind her in the recesses of the forest a thousand pairs of eyes staring back at her.

She didn't need another invitation to run. Picking up speed she covered the distance between the edge of the wood and the base of the twisted castle like an Olympic sprinter. As she ran through the force field, she heard a loud popping sound in her ears and then she was on the other side.

Nadia slowed to a walk and regarded the ivy and deep indigo blooms intertwining up the base of the building with the brickwork. It was like they were one and the same. Alar flew up to her nose and perched on her shoulder.

"Now we are safe," the bird said. "Let's get you inside and then I can explain everything."

"Well first I'm quite keen to know about how you can talk," demanded Nadia. "That would be a good place to start. And then you can tell me where the bloody hell am I? Like, I know I'm missing double maths and that's pretty handy. But this is crazy."

She glared at the hummingbird with a haughty expression.

Alar gave what could only be interpreted as a laugh and then said, "Yes, it will all be revealed. Let's get you inside! Absolon is waiting for you in the Tower of Sikuli. I know this must be very, very strange. But you will soon know exactly why you are here."

"Where exactly is here?" demanded Nadia.

"Why, Amaris of course!" Alar tweeted back with a chirrup.

"We've been waiting for you for such a long time. And soon you won't be on your own either. You have a very important job to do Nadia. All of our lives depend on it."

"No pressure then," grumbled Nadia under her breath while trudging up to the base of the tower. As she moved closer a door appeared out of the brickwork and swung inward. "Like seriously, is this for real?" she asked no one in particular and walked through the entrance.

Nadia made her way up a narrow winding staircase. She was aware of gentle whispering as she climbed the steps. The walls were engraved, and the markings, which looked like some kind of ancient language, shifted and moved.

Alar kept up a buzzing commentary as she trudged up the steps. "You are looking at the history of Amaris. It tells the story of our past and our destiny. The humming you can hear are the voices of our ancestors. They are welcoming you. Their spirit is imbued in these walls."

"I have to ask you how come you can talk? I mean that's one of a thousand questions but that's a pretty important one."

"You have the ability to understand us. It will not be the way with all creatures, but you will be able to understand many of them here on Amaris," explained Alar as he flitted in front of her.

Nadia reached the top of the stairs and found herself staring at the broad back of an imposing man. He wore a long robe the colour of midnight blue. Absolon turned and fixed his piercing blue eyes on her. Even though he looked incredibly old, he portrayed a sense of strength and magnitude. He also looked slightly terrifying.

Nadia was filled with fear. But it lasted only for a moment. Because when Absolon smiled, his stern look immediately disappeared, and his face was filled with kindness and concern. He walked towards her and opened his arms.

"Nadia!" he said. "I am so delighted to finally meet you. You have no idea how long we have waited. You are so very welcome to the Tower of Sikuli."

Nadia smiled back shyly.

"Hi!" she said in a small voice. "It's not often I am lost for words, but—"

Absolon placed a strong hand on her shoulder and said, "Yes, of course, you must have so many questions. And I will answer them in due course. But first," he pushed her away from him slightly so he could look her up and down. "No broken bones I trust? That journey can be a bit bumpy!"

"No, I'm fine. . . I think!" Nadia replied rubbing her arms.

Absolon nodded sagely.

"Good, good. Let me get you something to eat and drink. Travelling across the vast expanse of the universe through space and time can take a toll."

He clapped his hands, and a large snow-white cat appeared. Strapped to its back was a tray. On the tray was a large golden cup of steaming liquid and a plate of what looked like vegetable stew.

"Please sit down and enjoy," said Absolon as he waved towards the table.

Nadia's nose wrinkled and he took the tray and placed it in front of her while gesturing to a seat.

Leaning forward, she eyed the contents of the bowl warily.

Absolon let out a loud booming laugh. "I'm not going to poison you!" he said. "Whatever you want that to taste like, it will fulfil your heart's desire. I'm pretty certain you will like it."

Nadia gingerly took the cup and sniffed the contents. Her nose was full of the scent of strawberries, raspberries, and her favourite: McDonald's chocolate milkshake.

"How do you do that?" she asked before taking a swig of the foaming liquid. As it ran down her throat, she felt as if she had been given the most beautiful, tasty, and delightful drink she could ever have enjoyed.

No longer afraid, she began to dig into the vegetable stew. Nadia nearly spat it out as she took her first mouthful. "How does this taste like burger and fries?!" she asked incredulously.

Absolon wrinkled an eyebrow and grinned. "Why because we want to make sure you feel at home. You are a very special young lady, and we want to make sure you feel welcome."

Nadia smiled and then paused in her eating.

"Ok then. This is all completely mad. Like how am I here? How is this possible? What does all this mean? One minute I'm minding my own business and the next I'm on a . . . different planet. I mean, I don't even know where I am. And you are telling me I'm here to do something really important? I have to be honest, this is all completely crazy, and I need to know what on earth is going on. It does of course beat doing maths with those bitches who make my life hell." The words tumbled out of her mouth in a torrent. She paused and took in a breath. "But. This. Is. Weird."

Absolon looked slightly perplexed. "Well, I don't know what you mean by 'those bitches,'" he said. "But I don't take it to be a term of endearment. And of course, you must think this is very, how do you say . . . weird. So let me answer your many questions." He stroked his beard and narrowed his eyes, regarding Nadia with serious expression.

"We have brought you to our planet, Amaris, as we need your help. We are in grave danger from a terrible evil. I am what is known as a divine interpreter. This tower you are in is the Tower of Sikuli."

Absolon interlaced his fingers and leant forward. "My brother, Azvameth, and our two sisters, Allura and Allurea, worked with the different peoples of Amaris," he said. "Each had their own interpretation of the power of the Divine and respected how the universal force of Ruacha flowed and connected everything in our world. Despite our differences, we have always tried to live in harmony and with respect for each other."

Nadia was sitting on the edge of her seat listening intently to Absolon.

"A great and terrible evil came to our land," he continued. His eyes looked grave as he spoke the name of the evil, "Sathariel." Absolon walked to the window and continued softly, "Sathariel did terrible things to the people of Amaris. And she turned the head of my brother, Azvameth. He became obsessed with harnessing the power of the dark forces and using Ruach to become invincible. His heart was corrupted, and he now does Sathariels's bidding." Turning back to Nadia, Absolon continued. "She has now been in command of our world for 150 eons. But we always knew this curse could break, and she could be overthrown. The Yasha Prophecy fore-tells it."

He smiled at Nadia. "And that is where you come in. The heavens revealed we have a new leader. He was born to cure the rifts in our world and heal the hatred. He is the Chosen." Absolon looked at Nadia intently. "He can change the destiny of our world, but he needs help to do it. And you are that help, Nadia." Absolon pace the room as he continued. "You were summoned to Amaris through a Thura Gate, a gateway from one world to the next that transcends space and time. There are very few in this world, and those that still exist are hidden. Nadia, you are here because it has been foretold that you and three others of your kind will save us from this terrible evil. We are in a time of great darkness, and we must overcome it."

Nadia's stared at Absolon incredulously with eyes the size of saucers. "You think I can help?!" she squawked. "I'm just a teenager. I think you've got the wrong person."

"No, no!" Absolon exclaimed, moving towards her and gripping her shoulder. At the same time, he rolled back her sweatshirt on her arm. "See this?" he asked running his calloused thumb over the mark on her wrist. "You carry the mark. This is how I know you are the right person. You and the others of your kind who are coming to save us."

He then smiled kindly. "I know this is a lot to take in. But you are destined." Pulling back from Nadia, Absolon stood up straight. "Now I must summon my sisters." Taking a step back, he shut his eyes and pressed his palms to his temples. "Allura, Allurea," he called out. "Come into the safety of Sikuli."

Two women materialized on either side of Absolon. Immediately Nadia could see they were related yet looked very different. Both shared Absolon's strong features. He gestured to the woman on his left and said, "Nadia, this is Allura."

Dressed in a long, dark green robe, the woman stepped forward. Her eyes were violet and seemed to be deeper than the sea. Her pale blonde hair was twisted into knots which were intertwined with gold thread and green leaves. Her skin was like alabaster and glowed with an iridescence. She smiled at Nadia. "It's wonderful to meet you," Allurea said as she stepped forward. Her dress was shades of blue and slate grey, which reminded Nadia of the ocean, the crests of waves.

As pale as her sister was, Allura was dark. And her complexion also seemed to shimmer in the light. "Nadia, welcome," greeted Allura. "Thank you for coming to our home. With your help, we are going to help the Chosen win this war. So we can be saved from everlasting darkness."

4

"Who is the Chosen?" Nadia asked.

"He will lead us to freedom," replied Allura. "He will enable us to change our destiny. We know he is alive. But he is imprisoned in the Mine of the Malevolents. We have to free the Chosen and unite him with the Fylakistone, so he can fight the Battle of Ulpan La Inyan and finally defeat Sathariel forever."

"I really don't see how I am going to do this," asked Nadia, perplexed.

"Close your eyes and I will show you."

Allura beckoned the other divine interpreters to come closer. "Absolon, Allurea, come forward."

Nadia was aware of a hand being placed on each of her shoulders. But she felt like she was far away. She knew they were touching her, but she was looking down on herself. Then suddenly it was as if Allura was talking to her inside her head.

"Now we will take you back, through the eons of our beloved planet."

Nadia felt like the darkness behind her eyes was brightly lit, and it was as if she was watching a movie in her mind, like she was floating above the scene that was playing out before her.

In her mind, she heard Allura's voice. "Long ago, in our history, King Ciman and Queen Atropos ruled in harmony over our world from the capital of the Clan of the Elutheros, the Free People.

But they got greedy, and they got angry. They wanted power, and they turned to the power of the dark forces and became corrupted by it.

"Sathariel tricked them and made them make terrible mistakes which have led to our world being imprisoned. She promised them if they freed her from the Fylakistone, she would bestow on them riches and power beyond their dreams. But when they released Sathariel from the stone, she killed them and took over Amaris.

"The Elutheros who chose to follow her were transformed into the Legion, her soldiers. Sathariel then tried to take control of the Dragon Riders, the Caelum Bellator. To protect them, Absolon, Allurea, and I placed them under a protective binding Goitera, which shrouded them from being discovered and put them in a sleep. Incandescent with rage, Sathariel cursed the Lutrectos, the Elutheros's capital. All those who did not escape were transformed into the Revenir – destined to wander through the streets as lost souls forever.

"Sathariel knew that even though she commanded the dark forces, the Divine would put something in place to try and stop her. The Yasha Prophecy revealed the Chosen, the boy with the golden eyes, was destined to one day come and overthrow her. She knew that the goodness in the world, and the Divine, would not allow her to change the prophecy."

Absolon took up the narration in Nadia's mind.

"You see, wherever there is darkness, there is always light. And while many believe light to be the reason for darkness, it's actually the antidote. When terrible things happen, goodness comes in and mends what is broken. Even if it isn't how we expect it.

"The Yasha Prophecy tells of your coming. In our world, the evil power, Ruach, will be overcome by Ruacha, the good life force that runs through our world. The balance between the two will tilt. When the four stars appear flaming in the sky, they will bring hope and freedom. Then the Chosen will wield the Sword of Rajwa and the Shield of Aeras. And with the dragons by his side and the Army of Light, with the support of the four Yasha, and the Fylakistone placed in the hilt of the Sword of Rajwa, Sathariel will be overthrown. This is what we must see happen."

The movie that had been playing out in Nadia's mind went black. She was aware she was back in the room in the tower again. She opened her eyes wide and looked at them while nervously tugging her hair. "Ok," she said, jumping up and pacing the room. "So this is like, *waay* beyond anything I have ever had to deal with before. I'm not equipped for this stuff! "You're expecting me to find the Chosen, *and* beat off some crazy Malevolents, then retrieve a stone, get hold of a sword, and a shield?"

Turning to give the divine interpreters an incredulous look, her voice started to rise. "Oh, and you want me to wake an army of dragons and then kill and evil queen who happens to command the powers of darkness. Like, seriously?!" Nadia by now had her hands on her hips as she stared at them with an expression of disbelief.

To her shock, Absolon laughed. "You must overcome your own sense of disbelief Nadia," he said. "Do not fear. Have courage you can fulfil this quest."

Allura smiled kindly and said, "Nadia this must all seem very overwhelming. But we have faith. Faith in the Divine and faith in your abilities. Good will win out. And we will be beside you."

Nadia gave her a weak smile and nodded and said, "Okay, I kind of feel a bit better." She suddenly felt very tired. "I think I would like to have a rest before I start this 'saving the world' thing," she said. "Travelling across space and time is quite knackering."

Sensing her exhaustion, Allura laid a hand on Nadia's

shoulder. "Of course!" she said. "We have to wait for the others to come."

Nadia could tell Absolon nodded even though his face was in the shadows. He said, "However, if we know you're here, then Sathariel knows. And she will be doing everything in her power to stop you and those who are coming from your world. She is determined to keep Amaris held in her grip." Absolon clapped his hands together. The cat that had served the food and drink earlier padded back into the room. "Jeo please show Nadia to a bed so she can lay down."

Smiling kindly, the divine interpreter gestured for the teenager to follow. "We will send someone to wake you when we have more news."

As she left the room, Absolon and his two sisters watched her walk with heavy feet up the stairs. Looking after Nadia, Allurea asked: "Do you think she can do it?"

Absolon looked at his sister. "She has to do it," he said gravely. "She and the others are all the only ones who can save Amaris. Just because the Yasha Prophecy exists doesn't mean it will actually come true. And Sathariel knows it. We have no choice. If she and the others can't do it, then we are doomed."

---

*A*fsana found herself opening her eyes in a dimly lit corridor. Choking as she tried to draw breath, she only had a moment to readjust before Spark was talking to her.

"We must move *now*! It isn't safe here! Follow me!"

Afsana stumbled along the narrow corridor and managed to take in her surroundings in the low light. On the stone walls were intricate designs that showed scenes of people having what appeared to be a party. She could make out a king and queen being carried on a litter, with many animals and people rejoicing. This all passed by her in a blur as she blundered along the stone path.

"Where am I?" she asked between gasps.

"Lutrectos, the abandoned city," chirped Spark, as he buzzed to and fro.

"We must get to the Durara Gate. The streets aren't safe. But we can only go so far in this hidden passage. The final part we have to go up into the city itself."

"Why is it so dangerous?' Afsana asked.

"The city is inhabited by the Revenir. They are men, women, and children whose souls have been trapped by Sathariel. Until she is defeated, they have been bound by a terrible curse. And those that are lost have an insatiable urge to feed on the souls of the living. They will sense you when we go onto the street and will want to take you for their own. We'll have to be very careful crossing the city to get to the hidden passage where the Durara Gate is. Once we are there, the Revenir can't go near it because it is protected by Goitera."

Afsana didn't even question that she appeared to be having a conversation with a hummingbird. She was too terrified and confused as to how she could now be in this forsaken place.

Spark paused for a moment before flying in fast circles around her head. "We have in our favour that they don't like sunlight. Or fire. But once night falls it makes it very hard for us to make the journey, and for you to stay alive. I think we have arrived back at dusk, so we should have time. This way!" Spark hesitated, and then flitted over to a stone carving on a sun in the wall. "Push the center of the sun," he instructed.

Afsana reached out and pushed with her palm. The stone circle moved inward, and the stone swung away from her revealing a set of steps. Spark flew ahead and Afsana could see as she made her way up them that there was a door at the top. She pushed the wrought-iron handle, and the door opened onto a wide cobbled street.

In the waning light she noticed crumbling buildings lined either side of the street. The empty windows looked like yawning mouths, and ivy and other creeping plants had inter-twined through the brickwork. The street was deserted. It was clear this was once a bustling metropolis. But nature had long since started reclaiming it for its own. The grand boulevard was broken and uneven where the paving had once been. The silence was heavy like a suffocating blanket.

"The sun is setting, we have a few minutes," tweeted Spark. "You must run and follow me!"

He flew ahead and Afsana sprinted after him. They traversed the empty streets running past derelict shops that flashed past in a blur. Out of the corner of her eye, Afsana was aware the sun was plummeting towards the earth as it set for the night. She looked down and started to see tendrils of mist gathering around her feet and she pounded along.

"They are coming; quick, we must get there!" Spark buzzed round her head.

Afsana became aware of a whispering, and the mist began to feel like it was prodding her. It was now up to her waist. She could hear voices. "Help us, save us. Don't leave us."

Feeling like her eyes were playing tricks on her, Afsana thought she glimpsed shadowy shapes darting in the gathering fog. She let out a scream as she felt like a hand gripped her ankle. Afsana tripped and fell.

Anxiously Spark buzzed. "We are almost there. I can see the entrance. Don't look back."

And of course, as is always the way of things when someone tells you not to do something, that was exactly what Afsana did.

Through the mist, could see figures dressed in rags with bone white limbs lumbering towards her and staring vacantly. Afsana saw children, their arms outstretched, reaching out for her. They looked desperate and fearful. The whispering pleas were now like a keening in her ears.

"Don't abandon us. We need you. Just touch us, and you can free us."

Afsana was transfixed. She could not help but look in horror as a little boy stretched out his ghostly hands plaintively. His eyes were like black pits. Empty, he seemed to be staring at her with a haunted hunger. She felt riveted to the spot as the Revinir advanced towards her.

Her trance was broken by shards of light and fire piercing the mist. She could hear someone shouting her name loudly and with urgency.

"Afsana! This way! Run towards my voice."

Spark was whizzing around her head and dodging the flaming arrows.

'Come on! Follow his voice!"

As the fire rained over her head, Afsana heard blood-curdling screams.

"Don't hurt us, don't hurt us!"

The arrows of fire hit the Revenir, who recoiled and crumpled to the floor as they were touched by the flames. As Afsana ran full tilt towards the arrows, a man loomed out of the mist. He was tall and broad, shooting arrow after arrow which instantly sprung into flames as they left his bow. Behind him she could see a doorway lit by torches.

"Into the doorway!" the man shouted, and Afsana ran past him into the safety of the alcove.

Retreating backwards, Guilliaume, leader of the Elutheros, continued to shoot flaming arrows into the approaching Revenir until he was in the safety of the doorway. He then closed the entrance to the Durara Gate, sealing them into another stone corridor.

"Are you alright?" he asked a panting Afsana, who was bent double with her hands on her knees. She nodded. Guilliaume brushed himself down and slung his bow across his shoulders. "Good. As long as you are unharmed, and they didn't touch you. Not the friendliest welcome for you to Amaris," he said, smiling at Afsana. "Let me assure you that not every being here is quite as inhospitable."

Putting a large warm hand on her shoulder he continued. "Now we'll take you to meet the others. This next part of the journey will be much easier I promise you."

Nodding at Spark, the hummingbird settled on a notch on

his bow. Guilliaume gestured for Afsana to walk with him down the corridor. After a few minutes, they arrived in a large room. Looking up, Afsana noted it didn't appear to have any ceiling. In the center was a shimmering stone doorway.

"The Durara Gate. The fastest way to travel in Amaris if you know how. Luckily I have the key."

He grabbed Afsana's hand, and they walked towards the shimmering portal.

This transcendental journey was much faster and much more pleasant. Afsana walked into a wall of light, and within moments she was walking into a shaded woodland glade. She looked up and saw the sun glinting through the leaves of the tall trees. The doorway was the same as the one in the room she had left, with the exception the sturdy stone frame was covered in ivy.

Now they were standing in the sunlight, Afsana had to stop herself from blushing as she studied Guilliaume in more detail. His dark brown hair was pulled back in a low ponytail which made his green eyes even more piercing. With golden skin, to say he was impressive to look at was an understate-ment. Guilliaume wore a dark brown tunic, with a breastplate of burnished steel. His cloak was juniper, and he wore heavy boots on his feet.

"We're heading that way," he told Afsana as he pointed towards a meadow at the edge of the glade. "There is a twisting tower in the distance. Sikuli awaits. And there you'll learn why you are here."

"I really can't believe any of this is real," said Afsana. Suddenly she felt herself fighting the urge to cry.

"Pull yourself together," she chastised herself and pulled her shoulders back. Afsana then marched purposefully towards the meadow.

Guilliaume smiled. "I think she is brave, don't you Spark?" he said quietly to the hummingbird who was still perched on his bow.

bsolon, Allura, Allurea and Nadia were having a breakfast of eggs and toast when they entered. Nadia looked up and shyly smiled at Afsana who smiled back.

"Welcome, welcome!" Absolon said, opening his arms and beckoning her to sit down. "How are you Afsana? I know the journey wasn't an easy one."

"I'm good thanks. I'd . . . I'd just really like to know what's going on," she stammered.

Nadia stood up. "Hey! Apparently, we're going to save the world. So nothing major! Where are you from?" she asked, sizing her up a little. "You speak English. Are you from England?"

"No," Afsana replied. 'I was living in a refugee camp on the Turkish border when I came here. I can't speak much English. So, this is weird I can understand you."

Absolon smiled and said, "Ahh well this is what we hoped. You would be as if speaking the same language. So you can understand each other. One of the helpful side effects of the interspatial travel from the same world."

Afsana glanced at the plate of food. "Can I please have some breakfast by any chance?" she asked. "I'm like, starving right now!"

Absolon checked himself. "Yes of course, of course, my manners! Sit down and eat."

Nadia's face split into a grin. "Yeah, and he can tell you how we're going to save the world."

Afsana took a mouthful and looked at the teenager wide eyed.

"Ha, ha, no big deal, right?' Nadia shook her head slowly as she spoke. "This is going to," she said gesticulating to emphasize the point she was making, "Blow. Your. Mind."

5

"If you want to go for a surf before school, you had better get down there now!"

Yawning, Yibinathi rolled over in his bed and opened his eyes. Rubbing the sleep away, he pulled himself up and opened the curtains. His mum could always be relied on to give him a wake-up call. The sun was just coming up over the horizon and in the distance Yibinathi could see the ocean hitting the shoreline of Bondi Beach. The morning runners were like little black dots moving up and down the sand as they completed laps.

Yibinathi smiled to himself and began to fumble around in his room in the dim light to find his wetsuit. The only thing that made him happy about the fact his parents had moved to Bondi was he could surf. Being a black kid in the Eastern Suburbs of Sydney was not easy. His mum, Nomble, and dad, Ayize, both Jewish, had been worried about making the move two years earlier from their home in Cape Town. But the jobs they were both offered at Pfizer pharmaceuticals were just too good to pass on. Yibinathi knew he was going to have his work cut out for him to be accepted as a rich black kid who surfed. And try being a black Jewish boy in Sydney. Try being a black

Jewish boy anywhere for that matter. He needed to escape from the jibes and taunts at school because he didn't fit in. Anywhere. But out on the water, he could find the peace and tranquillity. In the ocean, he was at one with the water, with nature.

Yibinathi grabbed his board and leaving the house took the slow run down through the quiet streets to the beach. There were people already out on the water, bobbing up and down, waiting for the swell to build. The waves looked like they were building, and it was looking good for him to catch a few before he had to get back to get ready for school.

Paddling out, Yibinathi nodded at a few people he recognized as he made it out into the deeper water. He turned his board around and sat upright as he waited for the swell to build. The sun was already building in intensity, and he felt its warmth hitting his back. He turned and saw the waves rising behind him.

Yibinathi, who had surfed the Strand pipe at the Cape Peninsula, grinned and muttered, "This is going to be a good one."

He was a good judge of waves. Laying down on his board he began to paddle furiously. As the wave gathered momentum, exhilaration crept into his throat. He was at the tipping point. Yibinathi got into a standing position on his board as he waited to ride the break. At that moment he felt like he was flying through the air. The power of the water was beneath him, and he felt the rush of the wind on his face. That was when he saw it. While riding the wave he saw a tiny hummingbird just feet from his nose.

"What the?!" he said as the bird flitted in front of him.

He struggled to maintain his balance but was completely caught off guard. Yibinathi's feet slipped, and he tumbled into the churning water. There was a reason more accomplished surfers chose south Bondi to hit the waves. The currents and riptides were challenging and could be deadly. Gasping for air he felt his lungs fill with water as his board broke away from him. Yibinathi's body was plunged down into the dark water. He was turned around and around in the immense power of the waves.

This is it, he thought.

In those brief moments his life flashed before him. Yibinathi thought of his parents and his friends back in Cape Town. The kids that taunted him here in Sydney. This all happened in seconds. And then he opened his eyes and saw light above him.

No! he screamed in his head. *This is NOT it!*

Yibinathi clenched his jaw and managed to regain control of his flailing limbs in the churning waters. With all his might he started to pump his arms and push himself upwards. His lungs were on fire, and he felt like he wanted to choke and breathe at the same time. But the light got brighter and brighter. Yibinathi could see ahead of him a shelf – the ocean floor, which curved sharply upwards.

There's no shelf like that at the beach, he thought. *Maybe I got pushed out.*

His mind snapped back to the fact he was about out of air. When his feet touched the shelf, he pushed himself to the shallower waters and to the surface. Eyes closed for a moment, he sucked in oxygen between chokes. Endorphins, fear, and relief filled his body as he tried to slow his heart down. Chest heaving, heart thudding, he managed to slowly stand upright. Opening his eyes Yibinathi stared in confusion, bemusement, and wonder.

The ocean he had entered was definitely not where he was now. Yibinathi was standing waist deep in the water of a gigantic lake. He wasn't far from the shoreline, which was pebbled and sandy. He could see a herd of horses, their coats glistening in the sun as they grazed on grass growing at the water's edge. In the distance was a line of tents. There was movement and what looked like people bustling about.

Yibinathi began to wade towards the shallow water. Only after shading his eyes from the intensity of the sun, could he make out what looked like a man standing looking at him. He appeared to be beckoning him. Then he heard his name. "Yibinathi! Come!"

As he walked towards the man, Yibinathi began to make out his features. His skin the same color as his own. His hair was cropped short to his head. The man wore some kind of armour. Several knives hung from a leather band belt around his waist. He also had leather bands on his arms and legs along with gold bracelets and necklaces. He gave off an air of regality and strength.

As he got closer Yibinathi could see the man was smiling, which he took to be a good sign. Now standing just feet away, he stretched out his arms in a welcoming gesture. "Yibinathi, welcome to Amaris," the soldier said. "I'm Nakoa, leader of the Hayim, the Plains People. I'm here to protect you and make sure you get to your destination safely."

Yibinathi opened and closed his mouth several times not knowing what to say.

Nakoa smiled at him and laughed. "Brother, you have every right to be at a loss for words. Let's get you some food and clothes." He gestured and Yibinathi looked down and realized his wetsuit was torn into shreds and hanging off is body. "We will have to let Allurea know you're here, because it's definitely not where you're supposed to be. I know she will explain everything to you when she gets here," continued Nakoa, holding out his hand. "Luckily, I got word from the divine interpreters you were arriving in our lands.

"But tonight, before we go anywhere, we will rejoice. You have been delivered to us safely."

*M*in-Ji settled into her chair and adjusted her headset. It was the eighth day straight she had been glued to the computer screen. It was her only escape from her reality. In the online world she was able to truly be herself, to lose herself in an identity that nobody judged. She gazed out the window at the jagged Seoul skyline.

Calling up her skin, Min-Ji's fingers glided over the keys as she started moving through the virtual world. Going online, she saw her friend was already in the game.

"Hey Jun, how's it going? You know I'm going to smash you today?" She chuckled into her headset.

"Yeah, right. Here's hoping! You've got no chance," Jun responded.

'Ok, let's do this, I'm going to take you!'

Min-Ji, who was poised to move across the virtual land-scape in her skin, started running.

Ahead she could see a myriad of gems. Just what she needed to get enough points to get that blaster she needed. Suddenly, to the left of the screen zombies loomed into view.

"We've got to take this one together, Min-Ji," Jun shouted as they both wheeled around to confront the enemy.

"Yeah, let's do this!" Min-Ji squealed, letting out a whoop as they let loose a hail of fire that obliterated the enemy. She leaned back in her chair and blew imaginary smoke off her fingertips. "Nice one, Jun!" she said, smiling and high fiving the air.

Jun laughed through the headset. "Yep," she said. "I like working with you as a team more than as an adversary – mwah ha ha ha!"

Min-Ji smiled to herself and gave her body a silent hug. "Okay, I've got to move on. I'm SOOO close to getting that new blaster. Are you with me on this one, or are we splitting up?"

"Ahh, Min-Ji, you go on, my mum wants me to come to dinner," her friend sighed through the headset.

"Hey, why don't you get this hassle?"

"Ha, I have my ways," Min-Ji responded as she glanced back to the locked door.

Only last night her mother had been sobbing at the door, begging her to eat the third tray of food that had been left untouched outside. Min-Ji winced at the memory as she gazed at the corner of the room where clear bottles of dark liquid were stacked, reminding her she hadn't even left to use the bathroom. She didn't dare miss a second of the game. *No one understands this is where I can be myself. No judgement,* she thought.

"Hey, Jun," Min-Ji said. "No problem, all good. Catch you later. I have some more zombies to kill."

Min-Ji heard the click on her headset as Jun left the game. She opened her screen to see if any of the usual subjects were online. Not seeing any of the gang, she decided to do some serious gem mining, so she could increase her invincibility. Min-Ji's skin glided through the landscape, scooping up assets. In the game of Harab, she was invincible. She felt alive and happy. No one looked at her sideways in the street. She fit in. She was loved for who she truly was.

In Harab, Min-Ji didn't have to worry about what society put on her, the judgement, the anger, the disgust, the confusion. The burden she felt was so heavy some mornings she woke up feeling suffocated by herself. Some mornings she woke to soaked sheets because she had gone through so many anxiety attacks. Some nights her fear of shutting her eyes was so intense, she would run her fingernails down her arm until they split her flesh. She was so gripped with nightmares she was afraid to fall asleep. She would be lost in tunnels in the dark trying to just find herself. Her true self. Tunnels that never ended. No one knew who Min-Ji was, and although she wanted nothing more than for people to understand who she really was, she knew the world struggled with it just as much as she did. This was the only place she could be who she wanted to be.

Min-Ji blinked back tears and stared at the screen. She leant forward and blinked again.

"This is strange," she said to herself as she looked at a hummingbird hovering just in front of her on the screen.

Min-Ji moved forward, and the hummingbird darted forward. She moved forward again on the screen and stretched out her hand. She jumped as a voice in her headset announced: "Touch the hummingbird on the screen with your hand and go to the next level."

Excited, she leant forward and went to place her index finger on her computer. As Min-Ji's own skin touched the monitor there was a blinding flash of light. She felt every bone in her body shudder, and she thought her teeth were going to fall out.

She heard a voice in her head.

"Don't be afraid."

Then, an intense feeling like every bone in her body was being stretched to the point of snapping. Feeling like she was spinning through the air, the intensity was almost unbearable. Then as fast as it came it disappeared. Min-Ji felt like she was floating in a bubble in complete peace. She opened her eyes and saw the hummingbird in front of her nose.

"Don't be frightened," the hummingbird said, and Min-Ji didn't even flinch.

"Are you kidding?!" Min-Ji smiled. "This is the best immersive gaming experience I've EVER HAD! This is SOOO COOL!"

She laughed as the bubble she was in rotated in the funnel of light. Then, something caught her eye. Coming towards them in the funnel was a black object with snaking tendril arms of blood red and black rotating slowly. The arms were reaching out ahead as Min-Ji moved towards them in her protective sphere.

"Azvameth! Sathariel!" The hummingbird was flying frantically around the space in a complete panic.

Min-Ji looked puzzled.

"What? Who?

Then there was an almighty crash as she collided with the other sphere which quickly wound its tendril like limbs around her bubble. The hummingbird, who was called Glimmer, zoomed to Min-Ji's ear, wings whirring frantically.

"Sathariel has found us. Whatever happens, don't tell her anything. Even if you think it won't make sense. Even if you think it is something that can't help her. Even if you think it's something that will help you. She is a terrible, terrible being."

Glimmer then hovered for a moment before turning and flying with full force at the wall of the sphere they were floating in. Min-Ji screamed and in a second the hummingbird disappeared in a shard of light through the wall. She felt herself begin to gather speed as the dark red and black tendrils wrapped themselves around her bubble with a vice like grip. She looked in horror as they began to pierce through the thin film. They began to turn into sturdier vines and started to produce flowers that looked like indigo lilies. Min-Ji opened her eyes wider in wonder as the sphere began to fill with the vines and flowers. Each flower bloomed, and as the petals opened, they instantly emitted a pale grey mist into the sphere which was now almost completely engulfed by vines as it hurtled towards Amaris. Min-Ji felt fear for only a moment before she passed out.

Absolon was sitting at the table with a slightly stunned looking Afsana and Nadia, who was kind of enjoying the fact she wasn't the only person to have been knocked sideways by the news she had what seemed an impossible mission on her hands. Without any acknowledgement of how crazy the situation would appear to two teenagers from Earth, Absolon cleared his throat and began, "Now that you know the challenge ahead, Afsana, it's time for us to see the route you must take."

Allura entered the room, carefully holding a chest made of dark wood. It had jade and citrine stones embedded in a metal lattice which covered the lid. Not more than two hand spans across, there were two indents in the jewelled center which was in the shape of a sun. She carefully placed the small chest on the table in the center of the room.

"This is the Chest of Apokalupsis," she said. "It is a divine object, meaning the Divine himself blessed the process of making it. It is impervious to the Darkness and can only be opened by those which the Divine has deigned to have access. Allurea and I have been guarding the chest."

Her sister Allurea continued, "We have kept it hidden from Sathariel and her minions. The chest is covered with Goitera enchantments. Only Allurea and I can touch it, but we cannot open it."

She beckoned to Guilliaume. "Will you show Nadia and Afsana what we mean?" Allurea asked. "Don't worry I will heal you. I know you will feel the pain for only a moment." Allurea smiled and raised an eyebrow at the archer.

"You can take it Guilliaume. You are brave and have the stamina. Lesser men would weep!"

Guilliaume rolled his eyes at Allurea. But with a low laugh he walked over to the chest. "I know what I'm getting myself into," he said. "Anything to protect the fate of Amaris."

Allura, who was standing by, gestured for Absolon to take up position on the other side of Guilliaume, and they gently laid their hands on his shoulders. Spark ascended to a beam in the room so he could watch from above.

"Don't get me involved in this!" he tweeted to no one in particular as he zoomed up into the rafters.

Allura laughed. "Spark, we knew you would take yourself out of harm's way!"

Nadia and Afsana watched curiously as Guilliaume stretched his hand across the lid of the chest as if to push down on the metal sun to open it. In a moment the chest glowed white hot, and light beamed from the sun on the lid.

In the bright flash the two girls could see the fingers of light bloom out and wrap themselves around Guilliaume's hand and pull it towards the engraving. He squeezed his eyes shut and let out a cry of agony, "By Eloah!"

As the light wound itself around his fingers like a rope, the tips started turning black. The smell of burning flesh filled the room and his hand was on the verge of being reduce to cinders with the heat.

Absolon and Allura held the tall man's shoulders and uttered two words: "Ra. Les."

In a moment the light disappeared and there was an audible sigh as it dissipated.

Guilliaume gingerly opened his eyes. His blackened hand was turning back to normal. The skin which had been burned to a crisp became healthy flesh once more.

He flexed his fingers and stared at his recovered hand in wonder. "Well, that is a very good deterrent to stop someone who shouldn't be opening that," he said.

Allura turned to Afsana and Nadia, who were both looking from the chest to Guilliaume and back again with terror. "Okay, so you," Afsana said gesturing at the divine interpreters, "want us, to open that?" she said stabbing a finger at the chest. "And you think that won't happen to us?"

She glanced at Nadia, who was looking incredibly unimpressed by the situation that was unfolding.

Allura and Absolon nodded in unison. "We have every reason to believe this won't happen to you," beamed Allura, with complete confidence.

Absolon frowned slightly. "However, there is of course the caveat because you are not from Amaris, the chest could do something completely different. That we can't stop." He then smiled brightly and continued, "However I don't think that's something we need to be concerned about. I have every faith in the Divine and his unfolding plan.

"There's also the marks you have on your wrists which tell us you are destined to do this."

Nadia and Afsana looked at their arms and gasped as they saw they both had the same mark in the same place on their skin.

Allurea gestured as she explained, "You need to put your wrists on the indents on the lid. You are the key."

Nadia grabbed Afsana's hand and said, "Okay, let's do this. Don't think about it, just do it." They moved towards the chest and stood on either side. Afsana gave Nadia an emphatic nod, and Nadia said, "Count to three and we do it."

Standing either side of the box, the two teenagers intertwined their fingers so they could place their wrists down onto the lid at the same time. They stared at each other.

"One," said Nadia, and they moved their wrists down an inch. The chest began glow.

"Two," she said shakily, and they moved their hands down again until they were hovering above the lid, which was now beginning to emanate a blue light and shudder slightly.

"Three!" both shouted and slammed their wrists down on the chest.

There was a loud sound like a wailing chorus of voices, and the room filled with blinding blue light. As the noise subsided, the chest disintegrated into a pile of ash and on the table lay a scroll which was bound with a wax seal.

The divine interpreters gasped and then smiled and hugged each other. "It's true!" they said while laughing. "You've done it!" Absolon turned to Guilliaume and clapped him on the back as he punched the air. "Eloah be praised!"

They all rushed over to hug Nadia and Afsana who were shell shocked and blinking after being blinded by the light.

"This is the map to tell you where you need to go. It can only be read by you. It will show you a specific route you need to take which will keep you as far from harm's way as possible," Allurea told them.

Afsana picked up the map and broke the wax seal. Unfurling the delicate paper, she could see detailed forests, mountain ranges, lakes, and rivers. On it were lands with names she had never seen before. And she could also see two pins of pale blue twinkling light right next to a drawing of a tower, the Tower of Sikuli.

"Ahh," breathed Absolon in awe as he poured over the map. "So when you touch it, we can see the markings too. Nadia and Afsana, you are the blue lights on the map. Sisters, can you see the trail? It is showing they must travel to Myrkvior, the city of the Vanavasin, the Forest People. I am not surprised. Etan, who is the ruler of the realm, has been guarding the Fylakistone from Sathariel with the Vanavashtha."

Absolon tracked a red trail along the map to a vast forest. "It is protected by the Vanavastha trees," he continued, spreading his hand over an area of the map. "They're the gigantic trees that sing in a language which has been lost to us in the depths of time."

"So how are we going to ask them to give it to us if they don't understand us, and we don't understand them," asked Nadia, failing to hide the hint of sarcasm from her voice.

"Look!" Afsana said, gesturing to an inscription on the parchment. "It says what we need to say to them, and how to say it!"

Allurea gasped. "Wonderous! The map has concealed the translation from everyone except you!"

Absolon pointed to two other areas of the map. "I think we may have a problem. See here and here," he said, pointing at two other points of blue light. One was winking and popping and continuously shifting its position. "This is not good. The other Yasha are here on Amaris. But they are not where they are supposed to be."

Putting his hands on his hips in exasperation he exploded. "These damn Thura Gates, they are never accurate. We CANNOT let them fall into Sathariel's hands. For their safety and for the future of Amaris."

Allurea traced her finger a few centimetres above the map. "It looks like Yibinathi is near Qualea, in the realm of the

Hayim. My guess is, he has come through the underwater Thura Gate. I will go to them."

Allura, who was looking down at the map, drew a sharp breath and her face turned ashen. "But Min-Ji, I think we may be too late. I think Sathariel has already got her."

6

"Those Thura Gates haven't been used for eons," Absolon told Afsana and Nadia. "When we reopened them, we knew there could be problems. The reason they were shut originally was because the power to transverse time and space in the universe was just too difficult to manage. In the past people died, and terrible wars were fought over who was in control the gates. We were given the knowledge on how to reopen the Thura Gates, but by using them, there was always the possibility Sathariel would be able to use them as well."

Absolon sighed and then continued, "It was a chance we had to take. The price was too high not to take the risk. We used Goitera, binding enchantments, to ensure they could only transport you and you alone."

Absolon looked over at Spark who was sitting on the top of the bookcase observing them. "Did you know," he said, "hummingbirds are one of the only creatures that can transcend space and time?" He smiled at Afsana and Nadia and continued, "This is why they were able to come to you and accompany you back to Amaris. But the caveat is, they can only go on a direct route. That is, to the destination that is chosen and back again. They are in a unique position where the dimensions of a particular world don't hold them."

Afsana, nodded slowly. "How come we can't hear them on Earth then?"

"Because not every race is open to hearing what they have the ability to hear," Absolon said, smiling and nodding sagely. "Unfortunately, they like the sound of their own voices so much, the white noise they produce can tune out that which is right in front of them."

"You've got that right when it comes to humans," laughed Nadia.

She moved over to the map which was still on the table with the three glowing dots on it. "So if we are here and Yibinathi is there," Nadia said tracing her finger, "why do we not know about Min-Ji?"

Absolon looked grave. "This is my worry. Somehow, I think, Azvameth has managed to break through our Goitera and divert Min-Ji to Sathariel. He summoned all the power of Ruach to make that happen. If Azvameth *has* succeeded, he will obscure where the sphere has entered Amaris. We do not know the location of all the Thura Gates. There are some in the lands Sathariel has taken as her own."

Afsana, who had been listening but looking out the window suddenly gasped. "Look! What's that?"

There was a shimmering in the air at the edge of the meadow surrounding the tower. The vista appeared to snap, stretch, and bend in on itself. Then as if walking out through a waterfall, a tall woman appeared and started to run towards the tower. Her skin was sparkling in the sunlight. She was accompanied by eight hummingbirds which were glimmering too in shades of fuchsia and indigo. Holding a long spear in her right hand she sprinted towards the tower. The woman's long lilac hair was flying behind her. Afsana could see it was a mass of twists and braids interlaced with gold and silver. The woman's armour, fitted like a steel bodysuit, glistened in the light.

As she disappeared into the door of the tower, Absolon clapped his hands. "It's Imamu," he said," leader of the Spirit People, the Rehmat. This could shed some light on Min-Ji's location."

Nadia looked over at Guillaume, who seemed to be on edge.

Absolon frowned. "Now is not the time to allow eon's old suspicion take hold Guilliaume. We have a common enemy now."

Guilliaume tucked his hair behind his ear and rolled his eyes. "Yes, yes. For the good of Amaris. But it doesn't change my feelings, or those of Elutheros, about the Rehmat."

Entering the room, Imamu, who had clearly taken the steps two at a time, didn't even pause to take a breath. Grim faced, her jade green eyes flashed as she looked at Absolon, who already knew what she was about to say by her tense expression.

"Sathariel has Min-Ji," Imanu said. "The hummingbird Glimmer, who was accompanying her, was able to get out of the sphere. He believes Min-Ji entered Amaris at Azvameth's Tower of Sclymgeour and is being taken to the Dark Fortress."

Absolon slumped his shoulders. "It is as I feared. I was terrified this might happen. This means Azvameth and Sathariel are getting more and more powerful. If he was able to do this, then we must act as fast as we can. And Sathariel will know that Nadia, Afsana, and Yibinathi are here."

Afsana and Nadia looked wide eyed as Imamu turned towards them, bowed, and said, "Apologies for my abrupt entrance. Know that I, Imamu, and the Rehmat will do everything to get Min-Ji and Yibinathi to you. We have suffered greatly at the hands of Sathariel. Our people have been persecuted and targeted because of our ability to work with Ruacha."

"Haven't we all Imamu?" Guilliaume, who was leaning against the wall and observing her cooly, said.

The leader of the Rehmat gave the young archer a look of

disdain and continued, "By the power of the Divine you have my word we will be at your side."

Absolon gestured for Imamu to sit, and she took up a seat next to Allura. "The prophecy has always foretold the Chosen would come from the Spirit People," he said.

Imamu nodded and added, "Our children have golden eyes until they come of age, and then they change. The Chosen was destined to have golden eyes to see into the spiritual realm and the physical realm, so he could unite them. Since Sathariel came to power, she has sent her forces, the Legion, every eon to take our boys to her mines in a bid to find the Chosen and imprison him forever and in a bid to stop the Yasha Prophecy from coming true."

Afsana and Nadia both reached out a hand and touched her on the arm. "We are going to do everything in our power to save you all, and find the Chosen," Nadia said in a determined voice.

Imamu dropped to one knee and looked at the two girls, put her fist to her chest, and said, "Then as soon as you are united with Yibinathi, we will get Min-Ji back."

Absolon gestured for Guilliaume to join them at table so they could take a closer look at the map. "So this is the first part of the task that lies ahead of you," Absolon said, pointing to a mountain range on the parchment. "Here is where the sword is being kept, the Mountains of Elpis. It's encased in a pillar of adiaperastos. It's being watched over by the stone giants, the Hephaes. Once you have retrieved the Fylakistone, you will be able to retrieve the sword."

Imamu held up her hand, seeking permission to interrupt, and then said, "My people guarded the Fylakistone which has the capacity to hold the great evil of Sathariel. The Divine made the stone during the Dawning. But then it had to be split apart into three, in case the power it has fell into the wrong hands. The pieces were united and then Sathariel was banished from our world into the Fylakistone. It's part of the sacred rock of Sambandh. We always knew the Chosen would come from the Rehmat. So we always had a protector, if Sathariel somehow escaped. The Divine asked that every male child touch the rock of Sambandh in the first week of their birth." Imamu pointed to the marks on Nadia and Afsana's wrists and continued, "You bear the same mark. For the Rehmat, the mark left by touching the Sambandh would not be visible until a certain time in the Chosen's life, to keep them safe. But by touching the rock, when the time came, the child would be linked to the power of the stone and its protection."

Nadia and Afsana listened intently as Imamu took Afsana's wrist and rubbed her finger gently over the mark. "We have no knowledge how you come to share the same mark as the Chosen. That is the mystery and wonder of how the Divine works." Imamu smiled at the two girls.

Absolon cleared his throat. "So now, you know you will be able to find the Chosen," he said. "But there is one other thing you need to complete your task so the Chosen can overcome Sathariel."

Nadia looked at Absolon and Imamu and then back at Afsana, her face slightly stunned.

Imamu smiled and said, "Nadia, Afsana, you have the power of Ruacha, and the blessing of the Divine. You have me and my people at your side to help you with your task." With a sideways look at the archer, she added, "And you have Guilliaume and the Elutheros with you as well." Guilliaume allowed a small smile of acknowledgement as Imamu continued, "Yes, this task ahead of you may seem insurmountable, but that which seems impossible is what reveals one's true metal of character. That which you believe you cannot do, you usually can."

Allura nodded. "I have every faith in you," she said. "The Creator would not have chosen you and delivered you to us on Amaris unless you could do it. I truly believe you have the ability to succeed. You must hold onto that in yourself. Even when this going gets difficult, and you feel like you will fail."

Allura smiled at Afsana and Nadia with concern and continued, "You carry the hope of Amaris on your shoulders. And yes, it might be that all of us may not make it through to the end of this. Tasks of great complexity and difficulty always have casualties. But together we will be able to overcome what lies ahead of us no matter how hard that journey is."

Guilliaume stood up. "You have us. We are all with you," he told Afsana and Nadia, putting a hand on each of their shoulders. "This is the one thing Sathariel doesn't have even though she believes she has more power than us. Those who follow her do so by coercion. We are with you because we choose to be. And there is nothing stronger than loyalty born out of love, generosity, and free will."

Yibinathi walked towards the tents of the Hayim. Children were running around and laughing together while a group of women looked on, honing swords. The women all had their hair shaved on both sides, and they intertwined bright feathers and wove beads into long plaits on top. Their eyes were rimmed with dark kohl, and they painted lines of fuchsia and turquoise on their cheeks. With yet more bright colours on their eyelids, they were more vibrant than birds of paradise. Every woman had intricate tattoo sleeves showing off their long lean limbs. Wearing clothing fashioned from leather and suede, they all had tight-fitting jerkins, which had hooks and pockets that were clearly designed to conceal and hold weapons.

Yibinathi took in the scene of the camp. It was clear it was designed to be taken apart and moved at a moment's notice. All the structures were built of hide stretched across bamboo poles. The men were standing in groups talking, and they all wore leather and suede jerkins like the women. They also had feathers and beading, with mohawk-style hair and paint on their skin. But the colours were in shades of taupe, green, and beige.

"The Hayim women are at the front of the battle alongside their partners," Nakoa explained. "In fact, they strategize our attacks. Hayim women always know the best way to fight a battle. We teach the children battle games from when they are born. That way bravery runs in their blood."

Nakoa filled Yibinathi in on the Yasha Prophecy as they had walked back from the lake shore. A woman was walking towards them who looked different from the rest of the Hayim. "Ahh it is Allurea, the divine interpreter." Nakoa waved in greeting. "With Allurea's help, we will unite you with Nadia and Afsana," he told Yibinathi as she approached. "We will set off first light. It is Hayim custom to celebrate momentous occasions such as this." He slapped Yibinathi's back and smiled. "We are also preparing for war, and always have a gathering before a battle. There will be a feast in your honour."

Yibinathi suddenly became aware of how hungry he was. The idea of clean clothes and food sounded good. They had now arrived at one of the huts, and Allurea smiled in greeting as she pulled the cloth door aside.

"It's a delight to meet you," she nodded at Yibinathi. "Come and join us when you have changed. The clothing may not be what you are used to, but we do not have the same kind as you do in your home."

He smiled shyly. "Thank you, anything will do. I think this wetsuit has seen its last wave," he laughed wryly, looking at the shredded material.

Inside the tent, Yibinathi took a deep breath. He took in the thick fur rug under his feet and a large wooden bucket of steaming water. On the bed was a pile of clothing, a leather jerkin like the men were wearing complete with a set of knives. There was also a pair of the dark wool pants and leather boots. Yibinathi suddenly became aware of how tired he was. All his limbs were aching. He stripped off and eased himself into the steaming water, taking a handful of salts from a pot next to it.

As he rubbed the salts over his skin, he considered what he had been told. Never in his wildest imagination did he ever think this could, or would, happen to him. It was completely impossible, wasn't it? He pondered whether he could be dead, or in a dream. He stretched his hand out in front of him and touched the wood of the bath. No, this all seemed just too real. There was no way it wasn't happening. But he couldn't conceive how he was going to be able to fulfil the task that lay before him. He realized for once, for the first time in three years, he didn't feel like an outsider. He felt wanted. And he was needed. More importantly, he also felt respected. Yibinathi made a promise to himself. He would do everything in his power to fulfil the Yasha Prophecy. He pulled himself up out of the water and grabbed a towel. He dried off and then pulled on the clothing that had been left for him.

Arriving at the tent where Allurea had told him to meet them, he saw Nakoa was sitting crossed legged outside, slowly drawing on a pipe. The smell of cooking meat was filling the air, and some Hayim men and women were setting up tables. They were also working together to create a dance area as well as chop up food and cook the evening meal. The sun was slowly sinking into the far shoreline of the lake as Yibinathi sat down.

"We will be joining you when you make the final stand with the Chosen against Sathariel," Nakoa said quietly. "The battle is set to take place on the plains below our founding city, Qualea. Our people are destined to be part of the Army of Light. We have waited for this day, to banish Sathariel's evil from our lands." Looking into the distance he continued: "At the time of the Shattering, when Sathariel took Amaris in her grip, we had to leave Qualea and were cursed to roam until the four stars appeared in the sky." Nakoa's eyes flashed and with determination he said, "Now we can return home and stand at your side as part of the Army of Light." He turned and smiled at Yibinathi, his eyes now dancing, and gestured to the gathering in front of them. "Now, come, let us eat and drink. The time for battle is tomorrow. Now, we must celebrate your arrival. We have a long journey ahead of us."

Nakoa nodded towards the tables where a group of musicians had started to play a heavy beat. The crowd gathering was whooping and throwing themselves around with wild abandonment, dancing to the drums.

Nakoa slung a casual arm around Yibinathi's shoulders as they walked towards the growing throng. Some in the crowd were sitting at tables, tucking into plates of meat and vegetables. Allurea was talking to the women and helping with the children who were clearly excited by the impending party. As they neared, Nakoa clapped his hands to get everyone's attention. "Fellow Hayim!" he called out. "The time for us to return home has come. The Yasha, Yibinathi, has been delivered to us!"

He grabbed Yibinathi's arm and raised it into the air with his own. A huge cheer went up.

"By the power of the mighty Imani Mungu, we will come together with our fellow brethren and take back Amaris as our own." He gestured to the tables of food laid out in front of them. "But now, let us celebrate like it is our last night on Amaris." He pumped his fist in the air and continued, "To you, Yibinathi, and the Chosen!"

The crowd that had gathered let out cheers and followed his lead, chanting in one voice: "To you, Yibinathi, and the Chosen!"

7

*A*zvameth cracked an evil smile as he watched the mirror in front of him warp and shimmer. Rubbing his hands slowly he watched the sphere carrying Min-Ji hurtling towards him through the Thura Gate. It was completely obscured by the black, crimson, and dark green vines that were so thick they even suffocated the light.

Shaking his fist, Azvameth cursed with glee, "dark forces be praised, I did it. I diverted Min-Ji. Now, Creator, let us see if you can ensure the Yasha Prophecy," he spat the words out, "comes true."

The sphere was getting larger and larger in the mirror that covered an entire stone wall of the tower. It was Azvameth's way of seeing the world of Amaris and his connection to Sathariel without having to be in her presence. It was a struggle, draining even, to be with her for more than a short period of time. She sourced the life force of everything around her without even trying. You could feel the coils of her evil winding their way around your heart. The promises she breathed into your mind were enticing but deadly.

Azvameth shook himself. He held onto the promise of the power he would yield when she ruled Amaris totally. Then the divide in his soul from the continuous pull between Ruach and Ruacha would be gone for good. Then Azvameth could be at her side. Taking several steps back, he braced himself for the sphere to come through the Thura Gate. As it neared, his body began to shudder, and the mirror started to reverberate with light. Azvameth felt the spells drawing on his soul.

"Ruach be bound to me," he roared, feeling every cell in his being scream. The pain of the divergence he had woven impacted his body. Every time he used Ruach, it devoured Azvameth's very being. It was not like Ruacha. When Ruacha was bound with you, it felt like a comforting blanket, a loved one, or a friend you hold dear hugging you close. It supported you as it opened itself up to let you use it. Ruach, on the other hand, was all take, take, take. It took from your body *and* from your mind. But it was like a drug. Ruach was a cruel master. While Ruacha was a kind, loving, and nurturing friend, emboldening you to fulfil your life with all that was good. With Ruach you felt it was sapping the very essence of your soul.

Azvameth shook his head. He had devoted his life to the Creator, and Ruacha, and where had it got him? Nowhere. The promises and power of Sathariel, the dark forces, and ultimately what Ruach could offer, were far more beneficial as far as he could see. His selfish desires to be all powerful were satisfied by Ruach.

The sphere was almost at its breaking point now, just a couple of hundred feet away from the surface of the mirror. It was burning up with a red-hot glow. Azvameth started to scream as the Papaka, the enchantment he had cast, started to take its full effect. He reached out his hands and the tendrils of red entwined around the sphere started to shoot out of the mirror. This was the most important part. If Azvameth didn't take full control now, then the sphere would break free, spinning through time and space. Min-Ji would be lost forever.

Azvameth shouted out in pain and the tendrils latched themselves around his wrists. "*Veni ad me!*" he thundered and pulled the sphere towards him. Heat and light shot out of the mirror as the sphere prepared to split through into the reality of Amaris. "*Flectere voluntatem meam*!" Azvameth screamed again and pulled his arms down tight to his sides. The mirror burned white hot in a flash and then the sphere splintered through. The surface bent out as if it were a giant boomerang. Gripped in the power or two parallel realities, the sphere splintered through, breaking up and evaporating in a huge cloud of smoke and dust. A piercing light flooded the tower. Azvameth doubled over and started coughing as though his lifeforce was about to leave him. "How many more years have I just lost?" he asked himself as the smoke and dust began to dissipate. Standing upright he caught his breath.

Lying on the floor in front of him was the small, crumpled shape of a human. Min-Ji was curled up in a ball on the floor. Her short hair was messed up and her black clothes were covered in speckles of dust. Coughing and choking, she rubbed the dust out of her eyes.

"Where am I?" she managed to croak.

As she twisted around and pushed herself up to a sitting position, she could see Azvameth standing over her. "Welcome to Amaris Min-Ji," he smiled and held out a hand. "We have been waiting for you for such a long time."

She stood up and brushed the dust off her clothes. "Am I in the game? Am I in Harab?" she asked.

Azvameth looked at her in confusion. "No," he said, walking around her slowly so he could take her in from all angles. She looked so small and fragile. Was this *really* what the Creator thought could stop the power of Sathariel and the dark forces? To his eyes, she looked so weak and insignificant. Feeling slightly perplexed by Min-Ji's appearance and apparent vulnerability, Azvameth answered: "The computer game acted as a portal to our world. You came through a Thura Gate." Azvameth put a hand on Min-Ji's shoulder. "We have been watching you, Min-Ji. We know you are struggling in your world. You feel unaccepted. You feel no one understands you. How would you like to get rid of that feeling forever? How would you like to feel like you do when you are in the game all the time?" Azvameth smiled at Min-Ji as he continued. "I can help you find that peace you really want. I know someone who will give you that. Would you like that?"

Min-Ji looked up at Azvameth with wide eyes. Despite the fact she was feeling completely confused by everything that was happening to her, for the first time Min-Ji felt someone was offering her a lifeline. She frowned and looked around her. Ok, she wasn't in the game that was for sure. But she *was* somewhere else. Apparently in a different world. A world where she could be herself. Where she wouldn't be judged. And this man, who looked a bit like a wizard to her in his flowing robes and hatchet features, appeared to be offering her a great opportunity. Thinking nothing could really be worse than what she was dealing with back on Earth, she decided to embrace the weirdness of the situation and see where it took her.

"Yes, I would," said Min-Ji, wiping the remaining dust from her clothes. "I would like that very much."

Azvameth smiled. Min-Ji noted that it didn't reach his eyes. "Let me take you to someone very special. Sathariel can offer you your heart's desire. You never need to feel like you are an outsider or misunderstood ever again."

---

*N*adia shaded her eyes against the bright sunshine as Afsana, Imamu, and Guilliaume stood by the edge of the meadow. Allura was rearranging her skirts as she sat on a pure white stallion. Just a few feet in front of them the shimmering protective barrier warped and moved like the skin of a giant bubble.

Absolon adjusted the bridle of his sister's horse as he spoke. "While Ruacha is strong," he said, "Sathariel's increasing strength means the equality of the two powers is out of balance. It means Ruach is gaining strength as she spreads her evil in our world. This gives her more power.

"You must travel to the Forest of the Vanavasin and retrieve the Fylakistone." Looking at Afsana he continued, "We cannot use the Durara Gates too often. They harness a huge amount of Ruacha, and that makes the imbalance worse. Sathariel and Azvameth will also be able to detect where you are."

Allura gave a low whistle. Four horses cantered out of the forest towards them. They were already saddled and bridled with packs containing supplies on their backs. "This is truly the safest way to travel to avoid detection," she said, gesturing to the horses. "Once we are outside the sphere, we will have to use our wits more than Ruacha on our journey."

The tall black stallion in the group of horses cantered towards Guilliaume. His eyes flashed and he came to a stop in front of the commanding archer. Pawing the ground, he bowed his head. Guilliaume lowered his eyes and laid his hand on the horse's neck. "This is Akir," he said, patting the steed's neck. "Our horses choose us as their riders when we are five eons old. Then we learn to understand them through their behaviour, so we can communicate with them as if they speak. He and his brothers and sisters are honoured to be part of this quest." Pointing to the other horses he smiled at Nadia and Afsana, who both looked full of trepidation at the thought of riding. Guilliaume continued, "His sister, Keren will carry you, Afsana, and Nadia, you will ride on Lior. Remember, you ask them to let you ride them not the other way round."

Keren moved forward towards Afsana, who now looked vaguely terrified. "I've never ridden a horse," she squeaked.

The bay-coloured mare, who had a long cascading mane, put her head down low, and Afsana gingerly reached out her hand. Keren gently placed her nose on her palm.

"Shut your eyes," Imamu said, smiling, "she's trying to talk to you."

Afsana did as she was told and could feel a warmth in her

hand from the horse's breath. Suddenly she heard the words in her mind. "Know I am here to protect you. I will carry you to your destination and will spill my own blood before a drop of yours lands on the ground. Don't be afraid; I will only run fast if we have to!"

Afsana opened her eyes in wonder. "I can hear her!" she beamed and then smiled shyly at Keren. "Thank you, Keren, I will try not to be too frightened while on your back."

Nadia was jumping up and down. "This is amazing, we can talk to horses! Lior, come here and let me say hi!"

Lior, a dappled stallion rolled his eyes and snorted with derision. Guilliaume laughed. "He is saying he is honoured to carry you, but you need to show him some more respect. Lior can be a little grumpy sometimes. But he will fight to the death for you. And he has great knowledge of the forest."

"I'm sorry I didn't mean to offend you," Nadia looked down at the floor abashed. The stallion lowered his head and then looked up at her. She placed her hand on his nose. "No offence is taken," a deep voice sounded in her head. "Please let me help you mount."

Imamu swung up into the saddle of her stallion, a Palamino called Roi. "We need to get going," she told the group. "We have a lot of miles to cover before nightfall." She whistled between her teeth, and Guilliaume swung himself up onto Adir.

Absolon helped Nadia and Afsana onto their horses. "May the protection of the Creator save you from harm. And let your journey be swift and true."

With those words of blessing, Guilliaume leant forward and patted Adir twice on the neck. "Let's get going." Nodding at Nadia and Afsana, he commanded, "Hold on tight until you get into the swing of this!"

The girls braced themselves as the horses took off at a fast canter. As they felt the wind on their faces, there was a strange popping sound as their party pushed through the protective barrier. Nadia felt Lior say to her, "Hold on, we are about to go faster." And with that he increased his speed. She couldn't help but let out a whoop of joy as she felt the power of the horse underneath her. She turned and saw Afsana grinning from ear to ear while clinging on for dear life. The five horses neighed to each other as they lengthened their stride.

As they got into the rhythm of the gallop, and Nadia began to feel more comfortable, she started to take in the scenery around her. The tall trees of the forest reminded her of the huge oak trees near her home in south London. But they were so much taller. She was aware of the wildlife around her. She could see the hummingbirds flitting around Imamu, having no problem keeping up with Roi's speed. They took turns flying ahead to check out the way. After an hour or so galloping, the forest began to thin out as they entered grassland. The horses continued to keep up their speed as the high fronds hit their chests. Nadia saw there was not so much evidence of wildlife here, but she knew she couldn't shake the feeling of being watched.

The sun was nearly at its zenith, and it was beginning to get hot. The landscape was flat, and in the distance Nadia could see a copse of trees. Small clouds scudded across the sky.

Guilliaume turned back to the group and called out, "We've been riding for a few hours. The horses need to rest for a short while." He pointed towards the trees and continued, "We will stop there where we can rest briefly and have some water."

As the party neared the trees, Nadia could make out ruined buildings. The horses slowed to a walk as they came to the clearing. Guilliaume was frowning. "I don't like this. But we have no choice but to stop."

Imamu was brandishing her spear in her hand. She looked around warily. "Do you feel it?"

"Yes," Guilliuame said with a grimace. "Death." He looked this way and that. "I have a feeling the Malevolents have been here," he said to Imamu, who looked grim faced. "Curse them!" Guilliaume shouted. Then he paused as he listened to

Roi. "Let's get some water for the horses quickly. Roi says they are not happy here. They would rather press on."

The party dismounted and Allura opened her backpack. Gesturing to Afsana and Nadia, she showed them where there was a sack of water for the horses to drink and some fruit for them to nibble on. There was also a hunk of bread, water, and some sweet yoghurt drink for them. The hummingbirds were zipping around so fast their tiny-winged bodies were a blur. Guilliaume and Imamu were both on high alert as they ate with one hand and casually held a weapon in the other. Meanwhile Afsana and Nadia tried to bolt down their food as fast as they could.

Nadia looked at one of the ruined buildings. Its crumbling doorframe looked like a gaping dark mouth. She thought she could see something glowing in the darkness within.

"Hey Imamu," she said in a low voice. "Can you see that?" She tried not to draw attention from the rest of the group.

Imamu turned slowly and quietly said, "Yes, I see it. I think we are being spied on. Well, if that is the case, there is only one way to find out." She marched towards the doorway brandishing her sword. "Show yourself!" There was a long low screeching sound, and a huge black shape came bursting out of the rafters shattering wood everywhere. Its wings were oily, and its eyes were an icy fiery blue. It was a fearsome creature with a gigantic wingspan and nasty-looking hooked beak. Its talons could easily have ripped the horses in two.

Allura shouted. "Come stand by me NOW!" Nadia and Afsana scrambled to her side as the divine interpreter outstretched her arms. Imamu and Guilliaume shouted as they raised their weapons and the horses reared.

As the bird-like creature spiralled up, it began to change shape. Its wings melted into a black mist and began to rearrange into dark matter. Spinning in the air, it whirled around like a miniature tornado. The mist began to solidify into a creature in a ragged black cloak as it turned and began to descend on the group. With a high-pitched scream it began to dive down towards the party. It had no face to speak of, except for glowing white eyes. As it neared the ground, Guilliaume let fly a flurry of arrows. Imamu meanwhile held her spear aloft to stab at the creature's chest. It screamed again. Its bony white clawed hands outstretched as the arrows hit home. Stopping above the group for a few moments, it changed shape again, back into the birdlike being that had burst out of the abandoned house. It then flew up into the atmosphere disappearing in a dark blur.

"By Eloah!" Guilliaume swore, his face full of anger. "It's going to tell Sathariel and Azvameth where we are! We must get going immediately. We aren't safe."

Shaken, Nadia, and Afsana stared at Allura. "What was it?"

"A servant of Sathariel. No doubt summoned by Azvameth. It's a Malevolent. But it took on the form of an Obscura," Allura responded. "We must stay two steps ahead of her. There is no time to waste." Allura ushered Afsana and Nadia towards the horses.

---

*A*zvameth was pacing the stone floor of the Tower of Sclymgeour. He needed news. Now that they had Min-Ji, they had a chance of stopping the prophecy from coming true. *The stupid fool,* he thought to himself. It had been so easy to seduce Min-Ji with the promise of power and acceptance. Azvameth had seen into the world the Yasha were coming from to save Amaris. He knew it was as splintered as theirs was, just in a different way. The people of Earth had caused their own cataclysmic moment. He had read how they warred against each nation believing that their way of worship was the right way. *So many lives lost,* Azvameth thought to himself. Because they had allowed their own interpretations of the power of the universe to divert them from the true source of their peace and equanimity. This was exactly why Azvameth had turned his back on the Creator. A higher power that could not unify and control its followers was not worthy of his superior intellect. *Never mind free will*, Azvameth said to himself. *Free will never led to control and worship. And wasn't that what everyone wanted?*

Pacing the floor, his blood red robes swirling around him, Azvameth was convinced Sathariel could overcome the prophecy. These Yasha were ill equipped to save Amaris. They didn't understand the might of Ruach. And they also didn't understand Azvameth's power either. He walked over to his books where the Yasha Prophecy lay open.

Azvameth had spent so many hours poring over the document, trying to calculate ways he could bend it and stop what was destined from happening. It had taken every ounce of his power to divert Min-Ji. The strain was etched on his face. Azvameth appeared even older than before, his cheekbones even more angular and face more sunken. Catching sight of himself in the mirror, he winced. He knew if they could stop the prophecy and kill the Chosen, he would reign as Sathariel's most faithful servant. "Then I will be more youthful and more powerful than anything on Amaris," he chuckled to himself. The pain was worth it, as far as he was concerned. But it didn't stop Azvameth from turning away quickly from his reflection.

"Four to bind, four to mind," he muttered. "If we can keep one of them away from the others, they may not find the Chosen before we can imprison him."

There was a rushing sound as the Obscura he had sent to spy on Nadia, Afsana, and her party appeared in the middle of the room. Azvameth winced as his nostrils were seared by the smell of death that accompanied the Malevolent as it took on its true form. The creature's rasping voice grated on Azvameth's soul. "Master," he growled, "we have found the children. They are heading for the forest of Myrkvior. There is no doubt they are going to get the Fylakistone."

"Who did they have with them?" Azvameth demanded. "Was it still just the two of them?"

"Yes," rasped the Malevolent. "But they have Imamu and

Guilliaume protecting them, as well as Allura."

Azvameth was intrigued. The leader of the Elutheros and the Rehmat together? These two peoples had been at each other's throats for eons.

He frowned. "How do they know how to retrieve the Fylakistone? This makes no sense to me. How do they know where to go?" Then he realized. They must have opened the Chest of Apokalupsis.

Azvameth shouted in rage. "The Creator be damned! Having Min-Ji is just one aspect of disrupting the prophecy. But we cannot kill Min-Ji. We need to crush the Chosen and take the Fylakistone. Only then will Sathariel come to power."

He turned back to the Malevolent. "We must find the third Yasha. I cannot see where they are as their presence is obscured from me. We must prevent that meeting between them. At, All. Costs."

The Malevolent bowed and disintegrated into thin air. Azvameth stalked over to the open window full of frustration. Gazing out across the bleak vista, he knew he was incapacitated by the Creator. The landscape below him was volcanic and rocky. Azvameth had sucked the life out of every living thing within the shadow of the Tower of Sclymgeour in a bid to harness the power of Ruach. Rocky outcrops, dead trees, and empty riverbeds had replaced the once lush and pleasant land that had surrounded the Tower. The earth itself had splintered, and rivulets of lava now ran through what used to be green forests and rivers. Not a living thing could be seen for miles. And the earth was bathed in a watery half-light. However barren the landscape, Azvameth did not regret his decision.

"Creator, you turned your back on me," he said as his eyes filled with tears of rage. "You did not allow me to fulfil my destiny as the only divine interpreter for Amaris."

Looking to the sky he shouted. "This is why I take revenge. I deserved the power. This is why I will stop You and rule with Sathariel. Now I will take what is rightfully mine!"

Husam and the rest of the boys who were chained to him slowly made their way down to the bottom of the cavern. Winding his way along the pathways hewn out of the cliff, he could see down onto the floor where hundreds of boys were hacking at rocks. One of the Legion stepped out in front of him.

"Not you," he grunted and waved a disfigured piglike hand in front of Husam to stop him in his tracks. "We have enough. Now, you watch," the Legion commander Haigan said, letting out a disgusting snorting laugh. A horn was sounded and Husam could see Haigan on the mine floor.

"Listen all of you," he grunted. "Sathariel, your queen and rightful ruler of Amaris is going to bestow a wonderful honour on each of you. You have been chosen to join her mighty army. It is her way of saying thank you for the work and service you have given."

Haigan walked up and down the lines of dirty, bewildered-looking boys. "Now," he continued, tapping his whip against his thigh as he spoke, "you will have the opportunity to be part of the Reckoning." Haigan paused for effect. "Trust me. This is an honour our mighty leader Sathariel doesn't hand out to just anyone." Leaning into the face of one of the boys, he whispered loud enough to be heard by the ranks of boys. "You will be able to give your lifeblood to her cause." Those close by recoiled at the stench of Haigan's breath overpowering them. Standing upright the commander addressed the cavern. "It is a gift to fight alongside Sathariel and bring Amaris to its true destiny."

"I don't like the sound of this," muttered one of the boys next to Husam. "I can't see this being anything good."

"Silence!" snorted the Legion commander, who roughly shoved Husam's companion against the wall. Haigan blew his horn again, and Legion soldiers pushed and dragged three lines of boys forward to assemble before him. Their feet chained together, they dejectedly shuffled forward. Husam had a rising sense of fear in his stomach, which he tried to choke back. The boys looked like lambs being led to the slaughter. Some trembled in fear. Others looked straight ahead, refusing to show any sign of terror. A few of the boys looked at the floor, too frightened to meet Haigan's gaze.

He looked down at them. "You are going to get to spend eternity at the side of Sathariel. You have been chosen person-ally by her to be at her side." Haigan continued, "Now you will feel the full might of the power of Ruach. You will never again experience the pain and hard work you have endured here."

Husam's gut twisted as he saw a glimmer of hope on the faces of some of the boys. Haigan took several steps back and smiled cruelly at the assembled lines of Rehmat youngsters as he told them, "This is your blessing from her."

Dark shadows began to descend from the cavernous ceil-ing. Husam started to shiver, and he could smell the stench of death. It was the Malevolents. They were bringing icy cold air and despair with them. Some of the boys standing in front of Haigan started to scream. Husam gasped in horror. The boy next to him clasped his hand. They had all heard rumours of what they were about to witness. They knew about the boys who went from the mines and were never seen again. But they had never seen with their own eyes what happened.

Three Malevolents landed on the mine floor without a sound. The boys in front of them were now openly weeping in terror. They stepped forward as one and took up a position in front of each line. Then they opened their cloaks and their arms appeared so long they could encompass the lines of boys in front of them. They had no faces; there was nothing but darkness and a pulsating light emanating from where their eyes should have been. As one, the three stretched up and then bent over the children. Their voices, if you could call them that, sounded like dust whirling in the wind, a scratching rasping sound, that was keening and soulless.

Husam, and the other boys, tried to put their hands over their ears as best they could while shackled together. But try as he might, he couldn't block out the terrible words. "Be blessed by the power of Sathariel's kiss," he heard as the Malevolents enveloped the boys in their cloaks.

Husam could hardly bear to look at what was happening as the boys were engulfed by the Malevolents. The moment seemed to go on for an eternity yet was actually over in a matter of seconds. It was as if time had been stretched and distorted.

The boy next to Husam kept his eyes tightly shut. "What are they doing?" he asked. There was complete silence for a matter of moments, then suddenly blood curdling screams. Husam could see thrashing under the cloaks.

"They're fighting for their lives," said Husam quietly, not daring to look up. Then suddenly, as quickly as the screams had come, the silence returned again. The Malevolents stepped back and drew back their cloaks. The red light from the cowls pulsed stronger than before, as if they had been invigorated. Their presence was more overbearing and their forms more solid.

The boys were still there. Yet, they were not. Husam struggled to fight back tears as he looked at the lines. They were all standing upright but motionless. All the boys' skin had turned a chalky, ice white, and their eyes were vacant black pools. They did not move or show any reaction. All of them stared straight ahead into the distance. The three boys were animated corpses. Their souls had been sucked out of them; their life-force drained by the Malevolents. They were undead.

"Behold!" boomed Haigan, gesturing to the rest of the boys who were all aghast at what they had just seen. "Sathariel has blessed them with the power of eternal life! Now they will serve her and never again feel pain. Is this not a wonderful gift?"

Looking around the cavern at the mass of terrified faces, he laughed loud and long. One of the Malevolents raised a scaly arm and the undead boys all fell into line. They did not make a sound.

"This," it rasped to the terrified boys who looked on in horror, "is how we will build the Army of the dark forces. Be thankful Sathariel is saving you so you can walk by her side in victory!"

The undead marched after the Malevolent as it glided to the opening which led into the adjacent catacombs of the mine. As they left the cavern floor, Haigan turned and spoke to the rest of the boys who had just watched the ghastly spectacle. "We will have another Blessing ceremony tomorrow at dawn. Now, back to work."

---

*Y*ibnathi felt his head nod into his chest again as he struggled to keep his eyes open. The rhythm of the horses plodding slowly through the marshland was hypnotic to the point it was making him drowsy. They had been riding for hours. The scenery had remained largely unchanged: wide open plains and marshland. The horses were unable to move too quickly because the footing was treacherous.

"One wrong step and you can get sucked under," said Nakoa. "But you have a fine mount in Emin. He is surefooted and knows the pathways well."

Yibinathi had been stunned when he'd laid his hand on the horse's neck and could hear him speaking in his mind. So many things were strange about this land. He was still reeling from what Allurea and Nakoa had told him last night. The party went on until dawn. It seemed his head had only momentarily touched the pillow when he was being gently shaken awake. Thankfully, he didn't need to think too hard on the ride as Nakoa was doing the hard work for him. The dark grey stallion had explained this part of the journey would be the most monotonous.

The Hayim had chosen to become completely nomadic and make the plains and marshlands their home when they were banished from Qualea by Sathariel. They had come to know the marshes like the back of their hand, which was just as well as it was the only way to get to the Vanavasin. The mountain ranges in the distance were inching slowly closer, but not nearly as fast as it appeared Allurea would have liked. She was on tenterhooks and continuously vigilant.

"We will be making camp in the next couple of hours," shouted Nakoa who was slightly ahead of their group.

At least Yibinathi had time to think. Allurea had told him he had been chosen for a purpose. He and the other Yasha each had a part to play in rescuing the Chosen. "What is it I can do?" Yibinathi pondered. He was obviously good at swimming and surfing. But he couldn't really see how that could come in handy. He could speak three languages. But that wasn't going to help him now. *Maybe it will become clear to me,* he thought.

He was also excited to meet Nadia and Afsana. Allurea could only tell him that they were both as overwhelmed and bewildered as he was. Thinking back to his conversation with Allurea, it was almost as if they faced many of the same problems as mankind did on Earth. She had told him about how the divine interpreters communicated with the Creator, but the different peoples of Amaris all had their own set of beliefs and interpretations. They each had their own names for the Creator, as Allurea called the higher power here on Amaris. Yibinathi had heard Nakoa call their God Imani Mungu. Meanwhile Allurea explained that the Elutheros referred to this being as Eloah. But Imamu, who was one of the Rehmat, used the term the Divine. And from what he could gather, they all thought they were right. Now they all had a much bigger problem to worry about. And Yibinathi had concluded that unless they all got their stories straight, they would have a hard time defeating the dark forces and Sathariel irrespective of him, the rest of the Yasha, and the Chosen. Yibinathi suddenly became aware that the sun was getting low on the horizon.

"Time for us to make camp," Nakoa announced. The group had come to an area of raised earth which rose slightly out of the marshland. Indicating they should settle on it for the night Nakoa continued. "We want to camp somewhere slightly higher than the marsh," he told the group. "There are nasty things in these waters that love to come out under the cover of night."

Emin slowed and lowered his head for Yibinathi to dismount. Nakoa pulled torches out of his packs and began setting them up in a circle around them and the horses. This will give us some protection,' he nodded at Yibinathi. "I will stand and keep watch."

Allurea beckoned Yibinathi as she began to prepare a fire in the middle of the circle. "We will only be taking a few hours of sleep here," she smiled at him as he approached. "As soon as the sun is up again, which is early in this part of Amaris, we will set on the journey again. We have to limit the amount we use Ruacha as we don't want to alert Sathariel to where you are."

Yibinathi nodded. The last thing he wanted to do was head into a trap or come face to face with Sathariel without the others. Turning to Allurea he asked, "Can you explain to me what the difference between Ruach and Ruacha is? I have heard it mentioned, and I don't understand it."

"Ruacha is the good half of Ruach," Allurea said. "It is the lifeforce of the world around you, if you like. It runs through everything on Amaris. There has to be a yin and a yang," she continued while gesturing with her hands, "two sides of the same coin. One side, Ruacha, is positive, affirming, designed for good. It blesses and creates with its power. Ruach is the dark side. It subverts and twists and manipulates. It is death and everything that is bad about the lifeforce. Everything living sits between the two forces. Some of us have the power to harness it. But by its very nature, Ruach drains and warps and strives to kill. When you use Ruach, you need to take another's lifeforce to feed your own as it drains your being. But Ruacha leaves you feeling full of joy."

Yibinathi nodded. "So why would people use Ruach instead of Ruacha?"

"Ruach offers empty promises," Allurea answered, "and it also offers the opportunity to dominate. The Creator designed us all to think for ourselves and have our own will. So we must choose what we want to follow. Ruach is like the most delicious drink you have ever tasted, but you know if you have too much of it you will be sick. But it is addictive; you keep wanting it. And even though you know it can destroy you, you still want it, yearn for it, and eventually need it." She paused and closed her eyes. She clenched her jaw and continued, "It devours you, and the only way you can stay alive is to keep taking it and using it over and over again. That is the only way you can stay alive without letting it consume you and turn you to an empty husk." Tears were pricking Allurea's eyes. "Azvameth was a great and powerful Interpreter. But he used his skills with Ruacha to bend Ruach to his will. It will still consume him in the end," she added with a faraway look on her face. After a moment she turned and looked at Yibinathi. "Sathariel was once a human like you. But she drank from the cup of Ruach so much, it turned her into a dark force herself." Allurea slowly shook her head and came back into the present. Smiling, she patted the floor next to the fire. "But that is a much longer story to tell. Now we must get a few hours of sleep so we can be fresh for the journey tomorrow."

<hr>

Yibinathi was having an amazing dream surfing the longest pipeline in his life, which was full of hummingbirds zipping in and out of the tube of water. He thought he heard them calling his name and then as he fell off his surfboard, he realized it was Allurea shaking his shoulder. "Time to go," she smiled. He got up and stretched and saw that Nakoa was removing the last of the torches.

Nakoa looked at the sun which was poking its head above the horizon. "Let's get going. We know it's highly likely we could be attacked. If we get as much mileage under our belt as we can and at least get off of the marsh plain, that will make our position a lot sounder."

The four of them started packing up the camp as the horses stamped their hooves preparing to move off. Yibinathi felt frightened and on edge. He looked around him as he mounted Emin. The stallion's calm deep voice came into his mind. "You have the best people around you to keep you safe. The Obscura are no match for Nakoa and Allurea."

The horses moved with more urgency now but were still trying to stay safe as they picked their way through the marshland. Nakoa was on high alert. His eyes darted back and forth. Yibinathi turned to Allurea who was riding alongside him. "Why won't Sathariel kill me?"

"She cannot because you are bound and not of this world," replied Allurea. "And there is a much greater prize for her if you join her. Your lifeforce is worth a thousand beings from Amaris. And your lifeforce can give her the ability to transcend from our world into yours."

Yibinathi nodded, as though he understood. "So this is why the creatures she's sending just want to harm me, not kill me?"

Allurea sighed. "Yibinathi, you must try and keep yourself safe at this moment. Our priority is to deliver you unharmed to Nadia and Afsana and make sure Sathariel does not get to you. The Obscura were good creatures of Amaris, beautiful gigantic, winged birds. But they became entranced with the power Sathariel had to offer them. She changed them and turned them into her slaves to do her bidding. They now can travel great distances in a moment if Sathariel knows the exact destination and are sent with the power of Ruach. I believe Azvameth will send them to the Thura Gate, and they will try and trace you across the plains. They can be killed, but their talons are poisonous. If they scratch you, the consequences can be deadly. There is only one flower on Amaris that can work as an antidote. Sathariel made sure they were all but destroyed. My sister, Allura, has some of the very few that are left."

"Look!" Nakoa shouted. "The edge of the marsh plain. The horses will be able to move quicker now as the ground will be more solid."

Yibinathi noticed the horses had indeed begun to move faster and with more confidence. The reeds and fronds stopped abruptly a short distance in front of them. and gave way to gravelly grassy terrain. It couldn't have come a moment sooner. The air was filled with blood curdling shrieks. Nakoa gave a low whistle. He pointed, "See there, Allurea, can you make it out?' He said under his breath, "Imani Mungu protect us, it's Obscura. Two of them. Azvameth must have detected us."

"Get to that rocky outcrop for cover," shouted Nakoa, and the horses wheeled to the left. They galloped as fast as they could, dodging this way and that. The Obscura were gaining on them, and the shrieks became louder and more piercing as they closed the gap.

"We're nearly there!" Yibinathi shouted as the horses

picked up more speed. The riders shielded their eyes as the spray flew up with the horses cantering at a fast place.

Yibinathi looked over his shoulder and could clearly make out the Obscura that was gaining on them.

"Allurea, protect Yibinathi," Nakoa commanded. "I will try to kill them and use Ruacha as a last resort."

"Yibinathi, we need to keep you safe," said Allurea urgently. "Nakoa and I will try and fend them off."

"We can't outrun it," grimaced the Hayim, pulling knives from his jerkin. They slowed the horses, and he threw a long blade to Yibinathi. "Now my friend, this is your first taste of the dark forces." Nakoa let out a laugh as she looked up at the sky and unsheathed another of his blades. "Come now show us what your made of!"

Yibinathi gulped, and he felt Emin in his mind: "Do not fear. We are here to protect you."

The Obscura circled and screeched as Allurea and Nakoa grimaced up at the sky. Allurea indicated for them to dismount. The horses formed a protective ring around them both. They reared up and pawed the air, snorting with anger. Yibinathi looked up at the screeching creatures wheeling above them. "They won't want to kill you Yibinathi, just harm you," shouted Allurea. "Or even worse, try and take you back to Sathariel."

The Obscura pulled their wings to their sides and dive bombed the group. Nakoa gave a shout and jumped into the air slashing his swords in a pincer movement in a bid to injure the Obscura. It shrieked and wheeled away as it narrowly missed the tip of his sword. Nakoa then started whirling a slingshot around his head, and let it fly at the creatures. One of the heavy stones hit true, and the Obscura wheeled up again in pain. But the other creature descended with its talons outstretched. It narrowly missed raking Allurea with its claws, and she managed to take a swipe at its wings.

"There are more coming!" Yibinathi shouted. He could see the dark shapes heading towards them.

"How many?" Nakoa, who was loading up another slingshot while stabbing his sword into the air, shouted back.

"Too many," gasped Allurea looking at the sky. "We *have* to use Ruacha," she shouted. "It's the only way we can get out of this!"

"No!" shouted Nakoa emphatically as she took another stab at the descending Obscura. It screeched again as Allurea and Yibinathi managed to just shield themselves from its talons.

"Nakoa, "you are one of the best warriors on Amaris," Allurea called out, "but this is a suicide decision. We must use Ruacha. It's too late. We have to do it. Losing Yibinathi is too high a price."

Nakoa looked at them both and then responded with anger and resignation in his voice, "Do it."

The other Obscura were bearing down on them. Allurea straightened herself and called to Nakoa and Yibinathi. "One of you stand to each side of me. When I shout, hold your weapons aloft. But don't do it until I say. I will embrace Ruacha as fast as I can, so we can minimize the reverberations. That way Sathariel might not pick up on our echo."

Yibinathi and Nakoa manoeuvred into position. The Obscura wheeled away. It was clear they were waiting for their back up to come into position. As they were joined by the other creatures their wings overlapped. Yibinathi looked up and gasped. The dark shape melded and warped into one huge being. Its talons were the same size as one of the horses. It began to descend upon them at breakneck speed. Allurea was staring up at the Obscura, grim faced and determined.

She held her left arm up. "Wait, wait," she breathed. The Obscura was plummeting towards them.

Nakoa stared at her and shouted. "When are you planning to do this?" he asked incredulously.

"Wait," Allurea commanded again and shot him a steely look.

The Obscura was just a few hundred feet above them. Its

screech was becoming deafening. Yibinathi could see the cruel hook in its beak. The dagger teeth. He could see the poison in turquoise blue on its razor-sharp claws. The Obscuras' eyes were a cloudy white fire. He was filled with fear.

Just as it seemed the Obscura was moments away from destroying them, Allurea bellowed, "NOW!" She raised her arms above her head and then looked to the sky. At the same time, she began to sing. "*Creator creatura ligate. Diabolum hunc! In virtute tua a creatura mundi huius accipere.*"

The Obscura started to scream. Its wings seemed to be paralysed. Like some almighty force was holding it back from being able to descend lower.

"*NUNC!*" shouted Allurea.

Nakoa and Yibinathi held their weapons aloft. Bright blue light, like iridescent fire erupted from Allurea. It transferred in an instant to Yibinathi's and Nakoa's weapons. The three stood struggling to hold their weapons up high. Allurea pointed the spew of flame directly at the heart of the Obscura.

Nakoa joined her in the chant. "*Nisi ab ipso. Creatore creaturam.*" The Obscura screamed and slowly the flames began to cover its wings. "Again!" shouted Allurea. She got to her knees as she struggled to maintain the beam of flame. She chanted. "*Nisi ab ipso. Creatore creaturam!*"

Yibinathi joined in, channelling his anger and fear against the Obscura. The creature was floundering in the sky now. The flames were licking its feathers. Then as the struggle became too much, it let out one, final blood curdling screech before folding its wings in on itself and exploding in a ball of fire. The group ducked to the ground to shield themselves from the detritus—ash, bone, and feather—raining down from above.

Yibinathi crouched down and choked as he tried to breath in the air that was now full of soot. He could hear the others coughing and choking in the fog of the destroyed Obscura. As the air began to clear, he blinked his eyes trying to make out what was going on. He could see a crumpled shape. Gasping for air, he realised with horror it was Allurea. "Nakoa," he gasped. "Allurea isn't moving."

Nakoa, who was lying prone on the floor, rolled over. Coughing, he sat up and crawled over to Allurea. Shaking her he asked urgently, "Are you ok? Can you hear me?"

Allurea lay there lifeless for a moment. Then her body, which was rolled into a tight ball, began to convulse. She rose to her knees and then put her hands on the grounds, so she was on all fours and began to heave and vomit a black liquid. After a few minutes she stopped and sucked in air. Nakoa offered her some water.

After taking a few deep breaths, Allurea said, "It is done," and attempted to stand.

Nakoa rubbed her back as the divine interpreter calmed herself. Nakoa looked anxiously as Allurea retained her equilibrium. "The darkness of Ruach, it's like poison when you try to attack it. Yes, sister it is done. But we have until nightfall to get to the Vanavasin."

Yibinathi stood upright and looked at them both. "Then let's do it."

9

Nadia and Afsana couldn't stop looking up. Above them the forest canopy sparkled and twinkled with an effervescent light.

"Nadia, look, can you see the creatures up there?" Afsana gasped in wonder as she looked at the furry animals jumping from branch to branch. Their fur seemed to glow. They chirped to each other, and their huge eyes shone as they looked down at the party. As they swung through the trees, they hooked their striped tails around the branches to give themselves momentum.

"They're definitely following us," muttered Nadia.

Imamu turned on her horse and laughed. "They're Keryx, messengers of the Vanavasin. They are pleased to see you! Your arrival is the most talked about event for eons."

"What? So we're like celebrities?" Nadia asked, looking pleased with herself.

Afsana sneaked a smile. "Hey, we're like the Kylie and Kendall Jenner's of Amaris. How about that? If only I could take a selfie with one of those," she said wistfully looking up at the creatures.

"Yeah, my TikTok would be blowing up right now if I could video some of this stuff," laughed Nadia.

Imamu, who was listening to the exchange, looked puzzled. "What are celebrities? Do they do good deeds and are known for saving people in your world? If so, then you most definitely are."

Nadia looked at Afsana and laughed. "Well, some of them think they are saving the world and believe their opinion matters more than anything else."

"Yeah," added Afsana, "Legends in their own mind," and the two teenagers burst into giggles, and their horses looked back at them quizzically.

Nadia smiled as she winked at Afsana, "Don't worry Imamu, we're planning to be a lot more effective than a lot of the celebrities we have back home."

The party continued into the forest, and the trees rustled and sighed as they passed under the giant arches of branches. The bark on the trees started to take on a glow of mossy green and dark blue and the leaves shown indigo and deep pink.

Guilliaume turned around to the girls behind him and said, "The Forest of Myrkvior is an ancient place. It is said Eloah planted the very first tree on Amaris in this spot and from it grew this forest."

"Don't you mean the Divine?" interrupted Imamu with sarcasm.

Ignoring the warrior and throwing her a sideways look, Guilliaume continued, "The trees in this forest are the only ones in our world that can communicate with each other. It is said they are among the wisest and oldest living things on our planet. They can absorb the sound of the creatures that pass near them."

Afsana rubbed her arms. "Is that the tingling feeling I have?" she asked. "It feels kind of prickly but nice."

Guilliaume smiled. "Yes, they are feeling you. They know you are good people. Sathariel and the dark forces cannot enter here. The trees have their own guard against her powers. They will only let you in, if they want you to enter."

Imamu nodded. "Guilliaume is right," he said. "If you are

not of good intent, you may find yourself leaving the forest within an hour of entering it, no matter how hard you try navigating it. The trees of Mrykvior make sure you never find your way through."

Nadia couldn't stop looking around her. Everywhere she looked the forest was teaming with life. The noise was deafening. What sounded like crickets, chirping insects, and birds were communicating in a loud chorus. Brilliantly coloured butterflies fluttered past them, all shining with a shimmering glow. "Why do the animals glow like that?" she asked Guilliaume.

Waving to the forest around them he replied, "they say the roots of the trees here are connected to the heart of Amaris. Any living creature that lives here for long enough and shelters in their branches is fed by the centre of the earth itself. It draws their lifeforce from the inside to the outside. It makes it visible."

Imamu's horse started to slow as the path they were taking through the trees began to slowly wind upwards. "Nadia, Afsana, look ahead," Imamu said. "We are approaching the city of the Vanavasin."

The girls could see the canopy was getting higher and higher and the trunks of the trees larger and more spaced out. Ahead of them on the path was a huge wall of ivy stretching from the leaves across the forest floor and up into the sky. At the base was a gigantic wooden door carved in gold embedded in the intertwining leaves. As they approached two beings holding spears stepped out of the ivy wall. It was the Vanavasin. There was a loud rustle and the girls turned around to see four more drop down from the trees behind them and land on the path almost silently.

Guilliaume dismounted and walked forward with his palms upward and outstretched in a submissive greeting. "I had a suspicion we were not making the journey from the edge of Mrykvior alone," he said with a smile. "Your ability to conceal yourself never ceases to amaze me."

The four Vanavasin bowed deeply and smiled. Their skin seemed to change colour in varying shades of green and brown so as to completely camouflage them when among the trees. Their large eyes had pupils in shades of violet. Carrying long spears and daggers, they wore circles of leaves made of silver on their heads.

"Welcome Guilliaume, Imamu, and welcome, Yasha," said the tallest of the group as he stepped forward. "I am Ameen, and we want to welcome you to Myrkvior. The Vanavasin are honoured to have you here. We could not let you journey without an escort. Even though the forest protects us, with Sathariel's growing strength, there was no knowing if she could send her servants to break through." Ameen turned and spoke directly to Nadia and Afsana. "Yasha, your arrival has long been foretold."

The girls smiled and nodded. Ameen walked towards the doors, and the two guards on either side pushed them inward into a high tunnel made of green ivy that shimmered with the same ethereal light. At the end of it was another door with two guards. As the party walked towards them, the doors opened outwards as the first set of doors shut. Nadia and Afsana gasped as they came into a wide clearing surrounded by the biggest trees they had ever seen. Hundreds of feet up, there was a network of walkways between the trees. It was an entire city suspended above the ground and under the canopy.

"The horses will stay here, and you will join us in the city," said Ameen as he pointed upwards. "Our capital is suspended in the trees."

"How are we going to get up there?" asked Afsana.

Ameen pulled out a horn and blew it. There was a sound of rushing wind as four giant birds came whirling down from the treetops. Their feathers were the colours of the rainbow, and their chests were rose pink. Each wore a saddle on its backs.

"The sapaksa will take us up to the city," said Ameen and

then let out a laugh as he looked at Nadia and Afsana's faces. "It's perfectly safe! You may even enjoy the ride!"

The two girls looked sceptical as the sapasksa nearest to them lowered one of its wings to the floor. The saddle had room enough for four people to sit comfortably.

"Just pull yourself up on the ladder here," gestured Ameen "and then swing yourself into the saddle. Once you get on, I will join you."

Afsana hoisted herself onto the bird's back and Nadia followed. Once in position, they could see there were footholds in the leather and rungs to hold onto. Ameen jumped onto the sapaksa's back in one fluid move. Then pulling gently on a rein leading from the creature's hood, he turned around and said, "Hold on!"

The sapaksa took flight in one jump, beating its wings hard. Nadia gripped the saddle with one hand and with the other held onto Afsana who was in front of her. She felt nauseous like she was on a fast roller coaster. The sapaksa's wings were strong, and as Nadia peeked at the ground dropping away, she had to fight the urge to vomit. Looking up, she could see the citadel in the trees above them getting larger and larger and didn't dare look down again. It was huge, a thriving city in the treetops. Huts and buildings were all carved into the trees themselves or suspended on the sides like giant nests. The Vanavasin were running between buildings on walkways. On one platform, a group was sitting cross-legged and taking notes. They looked like they were having lessons at what appeared to be a school. circled to land by the grandest building in the complex.

"Welcome to the palace of the Vanavasin," Ameen said over his shoulder.

Sathariel was ready. She smoothed her midnight blue dress to her sides and gazed at her reflection in the mirror. Now was her moment. She could feel Min-Ji coming near her. It was pleasurable and yet painful. Sathariel had known the very moment the other Yasha had arrived. They were bound by the same prophecy as she. Their fate hung in the balance with hers. The divine interpreters had no idea how intrinsically linked they were. And it had worked in her favour. It had taken every ounce of lifeforce she could obtain through the Malevolents to bend Ruach to her will with Azvameth to divert Min-Ji to her. Staring at herself, her high cheekbones caught the light. If anyone knew what she truly looked like they would recoil in horror. Sathariel used nearly as much power to maintain her appearance and hide the ravages of Ruach on her being as she did to keep up her slow suffocation of the people of Amaris.

She was determined not to let the prophecy be fulfilled. The Malevolents had come to her, and she had drunk from the lifeforce they had drained from the children in the mine. Sathariel knew if she could get Min-Ji on her side, she had a good chance of destroying the prophecy. Her features twisted into a cruel smile. She believed it would be very easy. Min-Ji was damaged. Her own world had rejected her. She was desperate to feel loved—and accepted. Sathariel knew how to project love. She knew how to instigate desire. She understood the need to be accepted. Hadn't it led to her taking her stand against the Creator long ago?

All she had wanted was to be seen as the most important in the Creators' eyes. She had been the most devoted. But the Creator would not see her as above all the others. So she decided if she could not be accepted, she would try and take power and control for herself. Because if you cannot be sustained with love, then you find something else to fill the void.

Sathariel knew the weakness of humans and creatures of the earth. Had she not seen for herself how the Creator had fashioned them to have free will? Giving free will gave license to make decisions. This, in her opinion, was the biggest mistake. Instead, she gained her followers by wheedling and persuading with outrageous promises, more than the Creator would give. Once they accepted her, she was able to do what she wanted with her followers. Because they couldn't go back. And if that didn't work, she would exploit that vulnerability and use force. The only race on Amaris she had been able to ensnare was the Rehmat. It was the Creator's biggest error to link her to the Fylakistone, because it allowed her to use them.

"It's almost like my Creator," she whispered with venom, looking up at the stars though the window, "you were giving me the chance to show you I would change my mind."

Sathariel turned away from the mirror as the Legion guard hit his sword on the floor to announce the arrival of Min-Ji. "Your most high Sathariel, Azvameth is here with the Yasha."

She turned and rearranged her features in the most welcoming smile she could.

"Sathariel, rightful queen of all Amaris, I have here with me the Yasha, Min-Ji. She is most honoured to meet you," said Azvameth, bowing deeply.

Sathariel walked towards Min-Ji, who was looking around at the room, taking in her surroundings with keen interest. She stared at the throne made of carved metal and thorns and was examining with keen interest the tall candelabras that appeared to be dripping with ice and stalactites. Leaning on her sceptre, Sathariel paused near a pit of fire in the middle of the room; shadows from the flames licked the walls, throwing strange shapes like twisted winged dancers.

"Min-Ji it is so wonderful to meet you," said Sathariel in a warm, sickening sweet voice. "You must be so tired from your journey. I trust Azvameth has told you why you are here."

She moved closer to Min-Ji, taking in the black clothes, short messy hair, and naive look of the Yasha. "You have a very special task to perform here on Amaris, and only you can do it," Sathariel continued. "You have been chosen above all others from your world. Min-Ji, you have been bestowed the honour of being able to rule this place. By my side."

Min-Ji frowned. "Well, that's a very generous offer. But, why me?" Sathariel felt a twinge of anger and swallowed it down as Min-Ji continued. "This makes no sense. Why am I so special?"

Sathariel beckoned for them to sit down near the fire that was roaring next to the mirror on the wall. "Min-Ji, I know you are very, very good at playing games, that you have found a way to escape the pain of your life right now in your world. You believe there is a better way, and you yearn for it. Here on Amaris, you can have that better way. In your game you rule, don't you? You are accepted and admired?" Sathariel walked slowly around Min-Ji as she spoke, drinking her in from every angle. "But, in your own reality, you cannot be your true self. Don't you want that? Wouldn't you love to have the power you wield in the game you play in reality? Do you believe in power like that?"

Min-Ji stared into the flames. "Of course. But in Harab, no one knows who I am. I mean," she looked down at floor, her voice cracking "I don't even know who I am." Min-Ji noted that Sathariel, despite having a cold air about her, seemed to be looking at her with concern.

"That power," said Sathariel, as she walked towards Min-Ji and gently touched her face. "That power can be yours. This is your greatest opportunity." She ran an index finger down Min-Ji's cheek and whispered, "Let me show you Amaris. You will see that the world where you are accepted is actually here. This is what you have prepared for. This is where you were destined to be."

Sathariel walked back towards the fire pit and gestured for Min-Ji to follow. She leant forward and waved her sceptre across the flames. They crackled and danced as they changed to an emerald green. As Min-Ji stared, she could see fields and trees and cities passing by as though she were flying overhead. "But this, this is like my game!" she exclaimed.

"Yes of course it is Min-Ji," smiled Sathariel. "Because that place in your imagination, that is yours. That is your place of comfort, where you feel welcomed and accepted. That is here. That place is a reality. And that reality is Amaris. The reason you have never felt accepted on earth is because you were never truly from it." Sathariel looked into Min-Ji's eyes. "We do not judge by gender or colour here on Amaris. We create our own races. We have our very own power you can use to create everything you desire, want, and need."

As she spoke, Min-Ji felt Sathariel's fingers close around her arm. She looked up into the queen's face. It felt like every aspect of her being was being sucked in slowly and rung out, through Sathariel's eyes. Every fibre of her body was humming in a strange way. It almost felt like the queen was ravenous with an insatiable hunger for Min-Ji.

"I am just like you Min-Ji," Sathariel said, looking into Min-Ji's face with a sympathetic expression. "Yes, you may look, and see what you think is a woman. But I am not a woman; I am not a man. I am Sathariel. The very definition of what I am comes from the sum of my parts. Do you not see you are above everyone by being not one or the other? You are both. Embrace that, don't run from it. Let me show you how to leave the pain and rejection you feel. Let me show you how you can be twice as strong by becoming what destiny is urging you to be."

Min-Ji smiled, and tears welled up in her eyes. "No one has ever made me feel like me. I am so tired of pretending and fighting the feeling of not really knowing who I am."

"Yes," breathed Sathariel. "If you join with me, I can show you how you can fulfil that destiny you have already created in your game. And make that real."

Min-Ji set her lips in a firm line and stared back into the flames. "Tell me what I need to do."

"Why, Min-Ji, it's actually very simple," Sathariel said with a smile. "For you to get what you desire, for you to get revenge on those who made you feel so *inconsequential*," Sathariel said, practically spitting out the word. "I can give you the power that you want. All you have to do is give your loyalty to me. Swear you will follow me." Sathariel leant forward, and Min-Ji felt that strange feeling of being prey, making her hair stand on end. "Is that not what you want?" she asked, with a wheedling tone.

Sathariel clapped her hands together and the window in the throne room was filled with mist. A picture emerged. Min-Ji could see herself. She was standing in a beautiful room with the most luxurious bed and furniture she had ever seen. A gigantic chandelier hung from the ceiling. Drapes made of the richest velvet cascaded down the sides of the bed. Min-Ji was dressed in the most stunning outfit she'd ever seen. Sitting on a chair next to her was a beautiful girl holding her hand. The girl's laughter sounded like tinkling bells. She smiled with love at Min-Ji. Then the door opened and four people walked into the room. It was clear to Min-Ji they were good friends. But as she looked more closely, something didn't seem right. In the faces of those who were staring adoringly and hanging on her every word, she could see fear. She realized they were there because that had to be, were forced to be, not because they wanted to be.

Yes, everything Sathariel had said to her about how she felt alone and rejected was true. And yes, she was angry. Yes, she was hurt, and yes, she was confused. She wanted to be accepted. But something deep inside of her told her that if she wanted people to respect her and accept her, she wanted them to do it voluntarily. Min-Ji wanted them to *want* to acknowledge and love her. Because what good was respect unless earned? What good was love unless given voluntarily?

Min-Ji suddenly realized she was in a dangerous situation. She recalled the hummingbirds' words, and when she turned to look at Sathariel, she could see there was something hidden.

It was like the queen wanted to devour her not see her as an equal as she had suggested.

Min-Ji stammered. "It's a very generous offer, but I'm not sure if that's really the way I want to do things." Feeling more emboldened as she leant into her truth, she continued, "Yes, it's true I feel alone. But what is the point of having people who care for you and love you unless it's real and genuine. I'm not sure if that's the way I want to do things. Although it's obviously a very kind offer."

Sathariel's eyes flashed with anger. "Are you trying to say you are turning down my offer?" she asked sweetly, trying to recover from revealing her true emotions, but it was too late. The veneer had slipped. Min-Ji saw it, and now she knew she had to get out of Sathariel's fortress. The queen stalked away from the window and sat down on her throne. She looked at the floor and then narrowed her eyes at Min-Ji. "Are you saying to me," she said in a low voice that ascended to a crescendo of fury: "that you DEFY ME?"

Then Sathariel became incredulous. "Are you trying to say to me that you don't want to take advantage of this world I am offering you? You stupid fool," she spat. "You have no idea what you are turning down." Recovering herself she smiled cruelly. "Well Min-Ji, I appreciate you may need some time to be persuaded. I think you need to consider what is best for you, given your current circumstances. Remember, you are all alone here."

Min-Ji gulped as tears formed in her eyes. Sathariel got up and walked towards her. Reaching out, she roughly grabbed Min-Ji's chin. There was no sign of the gentle caress she had given previously. "No one," Sathariel hissed, "Is coming to get you. So I suggest you think about what your alternatives are." As the queen turned to leave, she called out, "Let's see how you feel after spending the night in my cells." She clapped her hands, and a Legion soldier appeared. "Min-Ji needs to be persuaded that she would be far better off working with me than against me. We need to give her some time to think about her very, very limited options. Take her to the cells in the mines, and she can consider what's best for her."

As the queen stalked away, a hummingbird flew down from the ceiling in a blur of light. It headed straight for Sathariel, who raised her hand above her head in defence. "Get that thing away from me," she hissed, beating the air in a bid to fend it off.

It took just a second, but the mists in the window shifted, and Min-Ji saw what was really outside—a landscape barren and devoid of life. And as the deceptive power of Ruach slipped from Sathariel, she revealed her true self. Min-Ji recoiled as she felt a wash of evil flood over her that emanated from the queen. A yearning, keening greed that was like sharp nails running over the skin of her soul. As fast as she felt it, the moment was gone. But Min-Ji knew she had to escape.

10

*N*adia slowly opened her eyes, stretched, and yawned. Above her the light was shining through the canopy mesh of leaves that moved like seaweed fronds in the ocean. She still couldn't believe she was on another planet. Was she in another universe? Was she actually here and still back home at the same time? She didn't know much about quantum physics, but she did know there was some kind of theory where there were different versions of yourself or that the past, present, and future ran at the same time.

She pinched herself hard on her left arm. Wincing, she looked at the red mark on her skin. If it made her wince, then she wasn't in a dream. This was her ritual to remind herself she was awake. She pulled back the light woven cloth under which she had been sleeping, got up, and went over to put on a light pale green robe that shimmered in the light, which had been neatly laid out next to a pair of gold sandals.

Last night had been, well, crazy. Her mind was still reeling as she tried to remember everything. First, of course, she met Yibinathi. He had arrived at Myrkvior a few hours after them. Nadia still couldn't believe he was from Australia. Well, kind of South Africa, she corrected herself. And he had a calming air around him she really liked. Nadia had found herself feeling like she really needed to check her appearance when he walked into the room.

She was also thrilled to see Allurea again and remembered how lucky they had been with their encounter with the Obscura. Nadia shuddered at the thought. This world had some terrible things in it. But was it really any more terrible than some of the stuff on Earth? It was just different.

She had also briefly met Nakoa, the leader of the Hayim. He had returned to the plains to gather his people, so they could meet them at Qualea.

Today was a new day. It was the day she, Yibinathi, and Afsana were going to the Vanavashtha trees to retrieve the Fylakistone. Nadia was nervous. They didn't know if it was going to work. It was a strange feeling to have all these people installing their utmost faith in them. Of course, they didn't have Min-Ji, but they hoped that having three of them would be enough. Then they would be able to find the Chosen and get the Sword of Rajwa. Oh, yes, and the rest of it: wake the dragons, kill the evil queen, and save the world. Nadia actually laughed out loud at the very thought of it as she pulled her clothes on.

Things had been so different back at home. The kids at school had either ignored her or belittled her. They had said terrible things about her. Even when she turned thirteen and had grown tall, lost her baby fat, and ditched her glasses for contact lenses, her classmates still made fun of her. It's as though they had wanted to keep her in a box. How dare she suddenly start to look pretty?

She remembered one morning walking into the classroom and every kid fell silent. She knew they had all been talking about her. A whole class of bitchy girls. Nadia found out later what they had been saying. One of them had spread a particularly nasty rumour, suggesting she had been talking about her pubic hair. She recoiled at the memory. Of course, once that started circulating, people couldn't get enough of what was being said about her. She was a target of gossip that whole year.

Nadia had felt alienated, alone, and rudderless. The girls she had been hanging out with didn't really want to be friends with her. The "cool" kids wanted nothing to do with her. She was an object of ridicule.

Some days she would have panic attacks at the school gates. Some days she would stick her fingers down her throat, because being sick was the only way she could stay in control. She was filled with relief with every dry heave. Funny, she thought, she hadn't even given those girls, or being sick, a second thought since she had been dumped unceremoniously through the constellations onto Amaris.

Nadia laughed to herself, "If only they could see me now! A whole world waiting for little old me to save them." She would never know how she had got herself into this position, but there she was. She thought about Afsana and Yibinathi. Both of them had been through tough times too. Afsana had fled her homeland because of war. She had been living in a refugee camp for three years. Her father had been a successful doctor, but they had been forced to flee their home in the dead of night with nothing but the clothes on their backs. Nadia didn't know for certain, but she was pretty sure if Afsana and her family had stayed, they could have been killed. And Yibinathi, he had been through a bullying experience himself. His passion was surfing, yet he wasn't allowed to embrace it because he didn't match the stereotype.

Nadia was grateful that here on Amaris they could understand each other. Now all three of them were on a mission that they could never have even dreamed of. And one that they had apparently been pre-destined for. Nadia had always believed in a higher power. How could you not? The complexity and beauty in the world just seemed to point to something greater. And she didn't think that just because bad things happened it meant that such a "power" wasn't a good one. Humankind made its own stupid decisions. What sort of God would it be if you couldn't have freedom of thought? Definitely not a benevolent one.

All three of them were of course worried about Sathariel. From what they had been told she was a very powerful, evil creature. And that was, of course, the problem. Min-Ji didn't know anything about Amaris or about Sathariel. Could she be deceived into following the evil queen?

"Nadia, are you ready?" Afsana asked, appearing at the opening to her hanging bedroom pod. She smiled shyly. Her head was covered in green silk, and she wore a robe like the one Nadia was wearing.

"You. Look. Amazing!" Nadia said. "How do you feel?"

Afsana blushed. "I'm nervous," she replied. "There's so much riding on this. But I feel there's a reason we are all here together. Surely, we've been brought together so this has the best possible chance of happening, right?"

"Right!" Nadia responded, nodding emphatically.

The girls walked out onto the broad branches of the tree and towards a suspended bridge leading to a platform where the sapaksa were waiting. Yibinathi waved. He was wearing a similar outfit but wore wide green trousers and a loose shirt. They had been told the previous night why it was so important they dressed in special clothes for their visit to the Vanavashtha trees.

They were the oldest living beings on Amaris, their roots were said to run down into the very centre of the planet. It was said they were among the very first things the Creator brought into being. They were sensitive to everything around them, and to be able to move into the glade where they existed, you had to wear clothes that were created from their leaves. The Vanavashtha had to feel you were part of them.

"Communicating with them can be an overwhelming experience," Etan, the leader of the Vanvasin, told them as they ate their meal. "Imagine if you could read a thousand books all at the same time. The knowledge would be trying to get into your brain all at once. That's what it's like. It can be hard to cope with the initial feeling of being exposed to that. Some people find it overwhelming. Like their mind is being so stuffed full of knowledge it feels like it's being overloaded. You have to let it flow over you."

"Like when you're hit by a wave?" Yibinathi asked. "That first moment it's terrifying, but if you let yourself roll with it and let it do the work for you, you can find your way back to the surface."

"Exactly!" Vanvasin said. "The Vanavashtha hold the key to you finding the Chosen. They will give you guidance."

"What do we need to do?" asked Nadia between mouthfuls of what was the best vegetarian meal, what looked like the biggest salad bowl she had ever seen, she had ever eaten.

"You have to approach them with reverence—and open your heart. If you don't, you cannot hear them," said Etan.

"Nadia!" Guilliaume waved her over to the sapaksa. "Come on. It's time to go!" She ran towards her mount and was helped up by the archer.

They took off, and Nadia felt the rush of wind on her face. The treetops dropped away from them, and she squinted at the rising sun. The canopy looked like a deep green and orange ocean.

Guilliaume pointed to the north. "See where the trees change colour? That's where we're heading."

Nadia saw the canopy was a deep indigo and mauve where Guilliaume pointed. The area was about the same as the O2 arena near her home in Woolwich. From this distance even the leaves seemed to be shot through with silver and gold. As they flew towards it, Nadia marvelled at how beautiful this world was—in a very different way to Earth. It was like the colours were much more saturated. Maybe she was just able to notice it more.

They began to circle down in wide lazy loops towards the indigo trees. As they got closer, she could see the indigo leaves belonged to six trees that were vaster than anything she had ever seen. Their trunks were the size of four giant Redwoods all together. The sound of rustling seemed to get louder and louder as the approached. "They're talking to each other," said Guilliaume. "Get ready, it's going to get loud!"

As the sapaksa circled down through the breaks in the tree-tops the noise became deafening. The trees themselves were like nothing she had ever seen. Their bark seemed to pulse and glow with rivulets of molten lava.

"This is why it's believed they have roots into the centre of the earth," shouted Guilliaume in her ear.

The branches were full of hundreds of birds, and the air around them was full of butterflies. As they circled down towards the forest floor and the branches got thinner, the noise began to subside. Now the air felt thick and warm with energy.

As the sapaksa landed on the forest floor, Nadia looked down and saw the ground was covered in a lush carpet of the greenest grass full of daisy-like flowers. As she jumped down her feet sunk into the springy, cool ground cover. There before them was a huge circle of stones covered in ivy and dark blue and mauve roses that made an open-air temple about the size of half a soccer field. In the centre of wide circle of stones was an altar of sorts with steps leading to a circle of six saplings with pale pink and lilac leaves, growing about ten feet apart. The slender branches quivered and shone with a bronze sheen.

"To speak to the Vanavashtha, you have to go and stand in between the saplings and touch them," said Etan. "They're connected to the larger trees. They are one and the same. Lay your palms on the trunks so you and the trees are connected in a circle."

The three of them looked at each other anxiously and walked towards the open-air temple. The nearer they got, the lower the noise of the birds in the trees subsided. As they made their way up the stone steps to the saplings, all they could hear was the trees rustling in the wind.

Yibinathi, Nadia, and Afsana stretched out their palms and

touched the trees and positioned themselves between them. "What do we do?" whispered Yibinathi. "Do we say hi first?"

"I think we need to say the words from the map and then just, err, wait," said Afsana.

Nadia, who had scribbled the words from the map down on a piece of parchment, pulled it out of her pocket. Holding in front of the three of them, they read the words out together: "*Sumus Aperta Ad Te.*"

With that there was a roaring sound. The leaves of the trees above them began to sway as if caught in a hurricane. The colours in the branches of the saplings began to pulse and change. The heat from the bark of the saplings began to creep up their arms towards their chest.

"Are they going to electrocute us?" whispered Afsana with fear in her voice.

"I think they want to check out our intentions somehow," said Yibinathi.

The three of them held hands tightly as they stood firm against the intense wind. Guilliaume and Etan shielded their eyes and hunkered down next to the sapaksa whose feathers were being blown this way and that.

As the heat and light crept up their bodies, Nadia felt an overwhelming sense that something was looking into every aspect of her being, her soul and mind. It felt like she was being searched. "They're checking us out. Let's hope we pass the test." The feeling was tickly but not unpleasant. Then the moment was gone as the Vanavashtha appeared to be satisfied with their search.

Next, Nadia felt as if her whole being was flooded with light. She shut her eyes and as she felt a wave of information wash over her. She laid into the feeling of being connected to more knowledge than she could even imagine. Nadia had the sensation that past present and future were all one and the same. She could hear a voice in her mind that sounded like it was many voices speaking at the same time.

"Welcome to the Vanavashtha. We and the whole of

Amaris have been waiting for you. What do you want to ask us? Choose wisely, as you can only ask one question, and we can provide you only one answer. But know we cannot lie."

Nadia cleared her throat. "Vanavashtha, thank you for letting us speak to you. We need to know how to put the Fylakistone back together with the Sword of Rajwa, so we can find the Chosen."

The Vanavashtha sighed, and it sounded like a song sung by many voices at the same time. "Once you have the Fylakistone, and the sword, stand together at the point where as the sun rises it hits the snow. Let the rays touch the stone. You must say this phrase three times: *Bugan, Chabar Samani Aeternum.* This will fuse the stone with the sword and enable you to recapture Sathariel. And know this: now you have been one with the Vanavashtha, you will be able to use the map to seek the Chosen. Its mystery will now be known to you. So you will be able to find his exact location within the Mines of the Malevolents."

The trees around them began to rustle with more intensity. "Now that we know you are pure of intention, we can grant you the Fylakistone."

The stone under their feet began to glow. The rustling in the trees gained intensity. "Put your hands one on top of the other and place them in the center of the circle," instructed the Vanavashtha.

Nadia, Afsana, and Yibinathi looked at each other anxiously and placed their hands their hands inside a small circle in the centre of the large stone underneath them. The warmth coming through their feet was intense and into their hands was intense. Suddenly the small circle of stone gave way and disintegrated. They struggled not to topple over from their crouching positions. Nadia gasped as they looked down. There, where their hands had been, was a hole inlaid with gold. Inside was a citrine-coloured stone. It was half the size as her palm and inside was what appeared to be a swirling mist. "That must be it," she whispered reverently. Looking at the others for permission, Nadia reached down and took it out of the ground.

They all stared in awe at the Fylakistone. The trees sighed again, and the birds suddenly exploded into song.

Etan, who was standing watching the scene, kneeled and put his palm on his chest. "El-Shaddai be praised. The Yasha have the stone," he said.

Guilliaume bowed his head in reverence.

"The Vanavashtha send you good speed to succeed in your task," the trees said in their sighing voices. You will face heartache and loss and many trials. But each of you will discover something about yourselves you never knew possible." With that the warmth that had flooded their bodies dissipated and they all felt the Vanavashtha presence retreat from their minds.

"Phew," Yibinathi gave a low whistle. "That was insane! I felt like they were inside my body and head."

"That was a crazy and enlightening experience," Afsana agreed. "What do you think they meant by heartache and loss? I'm scared. Like, more than I was before."

Nadia frowned. "I don't know," she said. "I'm trying to work out what they meant about the sun kissing the snow. I hope we will work that out once we tell the others what they said—and we get to look at that map."

They turned as one to walk back to Guilliaume and the others. No one said a word as they climbed on the sapaksa and took flight. Afsana gripped tightly onto Nadia's waist.

"Are you ok?" she whispered into the wind. Afsana squeezed tighter as the flapping of the sapaksa's winds covered their conversation.

"Yes, I'm just-I'm just scared. I don't understand why we have been asked to do this. I don't understand any of this. I feel like this is a dream. I feel like I'm going to wake up. And then I realize that actually I'm not. This is real."

Nadia looked back at her. "I don't know you that well, Afsana. And I don't understand any of this either. But I do know you were chosen for a reason. I'm guessing you've seen some pretty tough things and had to deal with a lot of heartache with being made to leave your home. You've had to go from having a good life to nothing. I think you're way stronger than you think."

Afsana gulped back tears. She felt like her heart was hurting. Nadia was right about the terrible things she had been through, but she wasn't ready to share just yet.

Nadia looked at Afsana and continued, "I ask myself why I was asked to do this. Me, from a council estate in South-East London. Maybe we are all here together because we represent something. We represent that it's about more than just us. It's about putting differences aside and looking beyond that."

She was quiet for a moment as they savoured the cool feeling of the gentle wind on their cheeks. "This place," Nadia said, breathing in deeply. "I feel like it's a lot like home in a way. All these different people aren't really that different. They all think the same thing. They just look at it through different eyes. They have to come together to confront the common enemy. And if we can make that happen, then they will be all the better for it."

Afsana nodded into Nadia's shoulder as the sapaksa started wheeling down into Myrkvior.

"I mean look," Nadia shouted with a laugh. "We get to do THIS!" She punched the air as they descended into the canopy. She gave out a massive whoop and Afsana joined in.

Yibinathi turned and grinned at them both, as he laughed and punched the air too. "We got this!" he shouted, and the sapaksa let out a shrill war cry.

"For Amaris!" Guilliaume joined in.

As the sapaksa landed on a platform in the trees, they saw Imamu waiting anxiously with wide eyes. She came rushing forward. "Did you get it?" she asked.

Yibinathi jumped off his sapaksa and ran forward to grip her arm. "We did, Imamu. We did. And we are going to set your people free. You'll soon be able to see the sons of your people again."

Imamu's eyes filled with tears as she whispered, "Thank you." Then her face hardened. She raised her face to the sky and let out a cry that echoed around the trees. "Sathariel, here my cry. We are coming for you. Feel the power and wrath of my people. We WILL BREAK YOU!"

She turned to the group, her eyes shining. "We will be a force to be reckoned with. Now let this journey *really* begin!"

11

The elders of Myrkvior had gathered in the main hall that was suspended high in the trees. On their arrival, Nadia, Yibinathi and Afsana were greeted with a huge cheer. The news had already spread they had the Fylakistone. Allura had joined them, and the two divine interpreters were sitting with the Chest of Apokalupsis between them on a large table.

The three Yasha approached, and Nadia carefully opened the chest placing the stone inside. Then she unrolled the map. Everyone looked at the parchment and watched the images shift and move before their eyes. As the Vanavashtha had promised, they could now see the map in a completely new way. It sprang up in front of them three dimensionally with so much detail they could pick out trees and waterfalls.

Nadia grinned with excitement. "Awesome! Look at this," she pointed. "Here we are in the forest of Myrkvior." They could actually see the three of them, tiny figures, suspended in the city in the trees.

"Here look! This must be the Chosen!" Afsana said, pointing at a tiny golden yellow shape of what looked like a hunched over boy around their age.

The room fell silent. Allura and Allurea stared in amazement. "The Chosen," Allurea whispered.

Imamu pushed forward. "Damn Sathariel!" She shouted as tears of anger filled her eyes. "By the Divine, there are the sons of my people." She clenched her fists with frustration.

Etan and Ameen, who had been standing nearby, moved forward and tried to calm her. Guilliaume said, "Imamu, our people may have had their differences, but we will not stand by and see this suffering of the Rehmat go on any longer. We are not just here to rescue the Chosen. You have my word we will get as many of those boys out as we can."

Imamu stood tall and proud and gave a quick nod of gratitude in acknowledgement.

"Do you think we can see Min-Ji on here?" Afsana asked while peering at the three-dimensional mountains.

Nadia thought for a moment and then on impulse leant over and took the Fylakistone out of the chest. "Put your hands over mine on the stone and think about Min-Ji," she instructed Yibinathi and Afsana. The three of them did just that, and after a couple of moments, their efforts were rewarded. Yibinathi, who had been studying the map, pointed at another shape near to where the Chosen was.

Etan punched the air. "Sathariel has her in the mines. This is good news." He smiled at Nadia, who raised an eyebrow. "Now, Yasha, we can rescue them both at the same time."

Putting the stone and map back in the chest, they took up seats around the table.

"So, we know the Chosen and Min-Ji are in the Mine of the Malevolents. But how do we get in?" mused Afsana.

Etan got up and started pacing the floor. "There is a way," he said, "but the only people who know how to do it are the Taura, the Mountain People. Brin, their leader, can be tricky, but they will want to help us, I think. Their capital, Faesten, is deep within the mountain range of Elphis, where the mines are said to be located. They will know a secret passageway."

"That's not an easy journey," Guilliaume said as he

frowned.

Etan smiled. "On foot and by horse, yes," he said. "But by air and using a Durara Gate we can make it faster. However, we have to see how the sapaksa feel about taking us. Since Sathariel has ruled, they have stayed in the forest as it's so dangerous for them to leave the protection of the Vanavashtha."

"Do you think they will agree?" Nadia asked.

"Allura and I can weave some protective Goitera that will help shield them in the air," Allurea interjected. "The Taura will also be able to get us to the Hephaes, the stone giants who are guarding the Sword of Rajwa. They have been protecting its location."

Etan looked at the divine interpreters. "Part of the reason the Taura aren't the friendliest of people is that they take their task very seriously and for good reason. But they have good hearts."

"Ok," said Nadia. "What do we have in our way then? There's bound to be something, isn't there?" she asked, rolling her eyes. Yibinathi laughed at her sarcasm. Nadia blushed and quickly looked away.

Imamu, who had been deep in thought, made a suggestion. "To get to the closest Durara Gate we can use from here, we need to get across the sandpits of Ophis. It's a desert full of giant snakes. Do you think we can use the sapaksa?"

Etan shook his head. "The sapaksa won't be able to fly over it," he said. "The vapor that hangs in the atmosphere can also be poisonous if you are exposed to it for too long. The only way across Ophis is to follow a trail. If you deviate from it, you can die. It's completely inhospitable. And the snakes are deadly. However, we know how to cross. Once we have come out of the other side of the Durara Gate, the Taura can lead us to Faesten."

"No one other than the Taura can speak to the Hephaes," Allurea interjected. "It is said when the Creator finished his plan for Amaris, he had left over molten rock. He didn't want to waste it and decided to create the Hephaes from the very rock that makes the Mountains of Elphis. They are part of the very fabric of our world."

"You know how protective the Taura are of their relationship with the Hephaes," Guilliaume frowned. "They use them as their own personal army."

Allurea shrugged in response. "Yes, true," she said, "they are a private people who don't suffer fools gladly. And they have always felt the Hephaes are kin. They are protective of them, and so they should be. But this is different. Now, we *all* face the same threat from Sathariel. Even the Taura will not want to live under her power. Their leader, Brin, is more open minded than most of their race. If he sees the Yasha, he will know there is too much at stake. Even he cannot ignore what is happening. They can only hide away in the earth for so long."

Etan looked between them all. "So with the Fylakistone, the sword, the Yasha, *and* the Chosen, we will be able to wake the Caelum Bellator." He whistled. "Sathariel will know the of her reign is coming when she sees Absimil in the sky!"

Allurea turned to look at the three teenagers. "Absimil is the leader of the Caelum Bellator, the Dragon Riders," she said. "They have been in an enchanted sleep for eons. Sathariel knows that if we have them at our side, her chances of winning any war are vastly diminished.

Her sister Allura nodded. "The Caelum Bellator were a mighty race. Sathariel created an airborne curse to stop them," she added. "Once one of them was infected with it, not everyone demonstrated they had been infected by the curse. So nobody knew if anyone else had it or not. It also infiltrated the dragon's lungs, so they struggled to breath and exhale fire."

Allurea continued, "We decided the only way to stop them from dying out was to protect them with an enchantment of our own, so we put them to sleep. The only thing that can awaken them is the Horn of Awæcnan that Guilliaume has been keeping safe."

Guilliaume continued the story, "Yibinathi, it is your task to awaken them. The prophecy says the boy from the Yasha will hold the key to the horn. You come from another world, so your breath into the horn will trigger their awakening. Then they will be able to fly again."

Husam stared at the stone wall of the cell in front of him. He realized that if he didn't do something, he would become one of the undead. Fear clutched his heart. He concentrated on his mother's reassuring smile and felt a sense of calm. Ever since he was old enough to understand her, his mother had told him he had been born for a purpose. And he knew the best way to tackle the task was to take it in small pieces. So first, he had to save these boys. He had to save them from this terrible fate.

Husam was roused from his thoughts by a soft sobbing sound. One of the boys was crying, "I don't want to be that—I don't want to be that. I don't want that to be me." The boy stared at Husam with wide, terrified eyes. "I don't want to be lost forever. With no life, no soul. I'd rather be dead."

Husam reached out a comforting hand and placed it on the boy's shoulder. "Don't cry," he said with as much kindness as he could muster. "We'll get out of here. We can be strong. I promise you." He said it again with more conviction, "I promise you." Husam looked at the ceiling and uttered under his breath. "Divine, Creator, Eloah, Imani Mungu, Ar-Rahman and El Shaddai, hear me as I call all your names. We need to get out of here. We must get out of here. Give me the means to free myself and these other boys. I just know this can't be our fate. You won't let this happen."

He turned to look at the other boys. He uncurled the fingers of his other hand and looked down at the glittering, sharp edged stone he had in his palm. There were traces of blood on his skin, where its sharp edges had pierced through the top layers. "'No, that will not be our fate," said Husam with determination. "I trust in the Divine. The Malevolents won't take our souls."

The sobbing boy looked down at the rock in Husam's hand and smiled. "You took the akatalite!" he gasped.

Husam nodded. "When we left the cavern, I managed to pick some up without being seen. The Legion were too busy monitoring the boys on shift. With this, we should be able to break the shackles." Nodding at the boy nearest the cell door, he said in a low voice, "Keep watch."

Husam started chipping away at the metal around his ankle. The piece of rock began to glow into every corner of their dark cell. The other boys looked on in amazement. Then with a single stroke it cut through the metal. The shackle broke in two and fell apart like two halves of an orange. Husam looked up, and without thinking he pushed his hair out of his eyes.

"You're the Chosen," the boys gasped collectively.

"Your eyes, your golden eyes," the sobbing boy said pointing at Husam with wonder. "My mother told me about you when I was a child. She told me the stories of how the golden-eyed boy would lead us to freedom. How you would unite us against Sathariel."

Husam looked at them with a confidence he had never felt before. For the first time, he knew what his destiny was. Pulling his shoulders back, he gestured to the sobbing boy who was nearest to him. "Come here," he called. "Let's get that shackle off you. It's time to take back our lives, and Amaris, for our own."

---

*A*fsana looked up at the sky. There wasn't a cloud to be seen, and she could feel the heat from the sun beating down on her neck. The intensity of its heat went through to her very bones. After they had been met by the horses a few hours' ride from the edge of the sandpits of Ophis, the heat had gradually increased. The landscape had changed from scrubland to gravel. Trees became more and more scarce and soon gave way to strangled bushes and plants that looked like cactuses. Etan explained they had to wait until the sun reached a certain point for the path to become visible. "The reflection from the sand means you can only see it at certain times of the day," he said. "As soon as the trail is visible to the naked eye, we have to make as much progress as we can."

So they had to stand in the searing heat until the path suddenly appeared before them, like a ribbon of water running across the barren landscape ahead of them. Afsana leant forward and patted her horse Keren on the neck. "How're you doing?"

She heard the horse in her mind. "The heat is hard. But we don't have too far to go to the Durara Gate."

As soon as the trail was revealed, the group moved through the dunes and stony sand at a slow pace. The heat was almost unbearable. The horses bowed their heads and walked slowly and carefully following each other's footsteps. Every now and again, the twisted skeleton of a tree rose out of the ground and bleached bones of animals littering the ground.

Afsana pulled the hijab she had fashioned closer around her face to keep out the occasional gusts of sand in the air. The silence was occasionally punctuated by a slight rustling sound like a paper bag blowing across concrete. The dunes looked like waves in the ocean. Afsana squinted and could have sworn some of them were moving. Although the heat was intense, it did remind her of her homeland in a way. The ride gave her time to think. She thought about the night she and her parents had to flee. Bombs had been raining down on their town for some days. Her parents had agonized over whether or not they should leave. When they finally left, they got caught in a crossfire. Afsana remembered how her sister Fareedah screamed and pushed her out the way. She could see all too clearly her siblings lifeless body lying on the ground, blood slowly seeping from her wounds. Her mother who was nearby ran over and clutched at her sister, letting out a terrible wail. The sound pierced Afsana's soul, but they didn't have time to grieve. Her father grabbed them and pulling them away from Fareedah's body called out, "There's nothing you can do, my love. Allah has her now. We have to try and save ourselves." He choked back tears as he pulled them both away.

"I didn't even get a chance to say goodbye to you Fareedah," whispered Afsana as she touched the pendant around her neck. Her sister's smiling face came into her mind. The emptiness since that night consumed her. She had resented the non-Muslims who invaded her country for its resources and to convert her people. She had blamed anyone who wasn't the same religion as her, for her sister's death. She had blamed them all for the loss of her home. She knew it was unfair, but she couldn't help it. But after coming to Amaris, Afsana had to re-evaluate her thoughts. Meeting Nadia and Yibinathi and the people of this world had changed her opin-ion. She had no choice but to work with Nadia and Yibinathi for a cause that was for the greater good of Amaris. They had the same enemy. And she realized she liked them both very much.

Afsana was snapped out of her thoughts by Nadia's voice, which sounded loud in the quiet. "Can you hear that rustling?" she asked. She was slightly ahead and was twisting around in her saddle. "Are those snakes we can hear?"

"See there?" Etan asked as he pointed to the shifting dunes.

Afsana could see a rippling effect over to their left. Then she saw the snake's body moving through the sand. "It's coming closer. What do we do?"

In a swift motion Imamu took out the two long spears she had been carrying across her back. Guilliaume quickly placed an arrow shaft onto his bow. Etan took out his sword and Nakoa produced a scimitar. Allurea and Allura, who were at the front and back of the group, pressed their palms together and created balls of light between their hands.

"Yasha, stay together, we'll try and to hold them off," Nakoa shouted.

There wasn't much room to manoeuvre on the trail. The snake was getting closer, its body as thick as a horse. It reared out of the sand and towered into the air. Its tongue tested the atmosphere. Guilliaume let two arrows fly, and they glanced off its scales. The snake hissed in anger and plunged down into the sand. When it surfaced again, it wasn't alone. Another had come to join it. They both opened their mouths and showed their fangs. The feeling of the danger was charging the air around them like electricity.

Allurea and Allura gave a shout and then hurled their balls of light at the snakes. Their blows hit home, and the serpents let out cries of agony.

"Yes!" Nadia cried, clenching her fist. Imamu followed up by hurling her spears. She struck one of the snakes in the eye, and it contorted in agony and fell back into the dunes.

"One down, one to go," Guilliaume called out. He had already restrung his bow with an arrow.

The snake was now so close to them they could smell the rankness of its breath. It reared up and hissed and flared out its huge fans of skin from the sides of its face.

Allura and Allurea pelted the serpent again with balls of light. The snake winced in pain but kept coming. It dived into the sand and reared up again, this time right next to the trail. Nakoa, who was nearest, slashed at its scaly body with his scimitar. Blood began to ooze out of the creature's wounds, but it kept coming. Narrowing its eyes, the snake paused for a moment and then launched itself out of the sand. It threw its body over the party in an arc and then dived into the dunes on the other side of the trail.

Afsana realized it was trying to separate Nadia from the rest of them. "Move forward quick!" she shouted to her friend.

Nadia didn't need to be told twice and urged Lior out of

the way. The snake corkscrewed around and saw its plan had been foiled. Not to be outdone, it performed a pincer movement. Nadia screamed as she realized it was now cutting Afsana off from the rest of them on the trail. Etan jumped from his horse and somersaulted onto the serpent just beneath its head. It began to thrash as he hacked at its neck. Allurea and Allura were spent but were trying to muster up the power of Ruacha to hit the snake again. Keren was turning this way and that, as Afsana held on for dear life. They couldn't get out of the serpent's coils.

Shouting, Guilliaume knocked another arrow. But the snake had other ideas. Hissing and writhing as Etan continued to hack at its thick flesh, it pivoted to face Afsana and Keren. It plunged its fangs into the horse's neck. Keren whinnied in pain and Afsana stared in horror. She was trapped. She felt a rush of nausea as for a moment she stared straight into the snake's eyes, watching the life drain out of them as Etan's sword hit home. As Keren stumbled and collapsed, Afsana went down with her.

Allurea and Allura dismounted and stumbled. Nakoa, who had been thrown from the snake after delivering the killer blow, was picking himself up off the sand. Keren was lying lifeless on the ground. Afsana was lightheaded and felt odd. She blinked slowly and tried to move her arm. Looking down, she saw the snake's serrated fangs had caught her skin. She was pinned by one of the bits of bone sticking out from its fangs where Keren had been bitten.

"Afsana, your arm." Allura cried. "We must get you to Faesten as soon as we can."

Afsana stared down in bewilderment at a gash about three centimetres long, which was oozing an orange liquid. "I'm feeling a bit strange." Her voice sounded weak.

As the light began to dance before her eyes, and just before she passed out, all Afsana could think about was that she had paid her debt to her sister. She had saved another person's life.

Guilliaume had to bind Afsana's body to his so she wouldn't fall as they rode. In any other circumstance, she would have been delighted to be in this situation. Guilliaume was not much older than her but had a gravitas and calm that Afsana liked. As leader of the Elutheros, he felt a responsibility to his people far beyond his years. Ever since he had first saved her from the Revenir, she had felt a closeness growing between them. Now, she was literally bound to him, and she felt so ill she couldn't enjoy being that close.

All around Afsana, the landscape shimmered with a lilac hue. She could feel a chill creeping into every inch of her bones. She raised her head slowly, which felt as heavy as lead. Looking up at the night sky the stars seemed so brilliant and bright they were almost blinding. Raising her hand to her face, she could feel her hair sticking to her skin, which was clammy to the touch.

"Why do I—does my skin feel so hot, yet I feel so cold?" She managed to croak through cracked lips. With a great effort, she turned to look at Nadia who was riding alongside her.

"You are going to be okay, Afsana. We don't have long to

go," Nadia said anxiously. "We don't have too long to go to get to Faesten."

Afsana looked at her blankly. It was clear the poison from the snake was slowly getting around her body.

Nadia turned to Allurea and asked, "How long do we have to go to get to the Durara Gate?"

"About an hour," the divine interpreter responded quietly. "But once we get through it, we have only a short period of time before the venom completely takes hold."

Nadia glanced at Yibinathi, who looked just as concerned. The thought of losing Afsana was unbearable. Nadia was also well aware she had sacrificed her own life to save her. Tears pricked her eyes. "I will not let her die," she said with a determined look.

Guillaume, who was holding Afsana with care looked down and with fire in his eyes said, "You have my word she won't."

Ahead of them the desert was beginning to peter out, and the landscape was once again turning to scrubland.

Etan pointed to a rocky outcrop ahead. "The Durara Gate is just ahead of us," he said.

The party picked their way across the stones and the shallow slope until they came to a gateway in the rock. "This is the Durara Gate that will take us to the nearest point to Faesten," said Etan, gesturing to the pillars. We must enter as quickly as possible. Any ripple in the fabric of time is a calling card to Sathariel that we are moving."

They all nodded in silent agreement. The group entered the Durara Gate, and Nadia squinted her eyes as they passed into the semi-darkness. She could make out images and carvings showing scenes from some bygone age—armies marching and dragons fighting. Everything was lit by flickering torches. Nadia could see that the passage had not been used for what seemed to be hundreds of years. The images on the walls seemed to move in the torchlight.

Nadia glanced at Afsana, whose face was waxy and pale.

She was covered in a sheen of perspiration. It was a blessing she was unconscious.

"She's not good," Guilliaume said quietly, his eyes full of worry. "I don't know how much longer she is going to be able to hang on."

"We should be coming out of the gate any moment," responded Allura. "Then it won't be too far to the Mountains of Elphis. I can see the passageway is changing up ahead."

As they came into the moonlight the air was crisp and cold. They were surrounded by rocky terrain, with strange, twisted shapes in front of mountains looming like gigantic watchmen. The snow-capped peaks sparkled like crystals. A path wound up into the mountains towards a gash in the rock-face that looked like an angry open mouth. The horses picked their way across the scree towards the entrance, and the only sound was Afsana's ragged gasps for breath.

As they rode towards the entrance, two short, heavy-set figures appeared, wearing chainmail and armour. Their beards were plaited, and they held spears and shields.

One of them stepped forward and glared at the party. "Who goes there?" the Taura barked.

"Etan, the leader of the Vanavasin. We come with the Yasha; the divine interpreters Allura and Allurea; Guilliaume, leader of the Elutheros; and Imamu, leader of the Rehmat."

"Esteemed company, indeed," said the Taura, sizing them up with a long glance that swept over the group. He caught sight of Afsana, and his expression turned to one of concern. "Ah, she's had a tangle with an Ophis snake. How is she still alive? You're miles from there."

"We used the Durara Gate to get here as fast as possible," said Imamu. Her voice was tinged with exasperation. "We urgently need her to see a wisewoman to see if she can be saved. She is one of the Yasha."

The Taura's eyes widened. "One of the Yasha?" he gasped. "We cannot have her departing from us, no, no, no. That will never do. Not under the watch of the Taura." Turning to his companion, he said, "Go ahead to Brin and tell them our guests are on the way. And alert the wisewoman."

He stood aside and ushered the group to follow him into the mountain.

Yibinathi was beginning to wonder if they were ever going to get to their destination. He was desperately worried about Afsana. The group had been riding for some minutes along winding passages through the rock. The Taura walked ahead of them. The corridor through the rock was slowly getting wider. One of the Taura who had been guiding them from the entrance paused and held up his hand. "We are about to enter Faesten. You will be completely safe here. Sathariel cannot touch you. We have been bound by Goitera, so only those who we allow to see us are able to find our city."

As Yibinathi looked at the sight before him, his jaw hit the floor. The mountain they were standing inside was hollow. Yibinathi was staring at the largest, most vast cavern he had ever seen. And inside it was an entire city. Lights twinkled and glittered from buildings and streets that lined the cavern floor and climbed up the walls. The structures were hewn out of the rock and were part of the mountain. As his eyes adjusted, Yibinathi could see the glow of deep fire pits, streets bustling with life as the Taura bustled about their business. He realized the twinkling was coming from gemstones glittering in the walls of the buildings.

"Welcome to Faesten," said the Taura proudly. "Now, let's get the Yasha to the wisewoman immediately. We must make haste."

As they made their way down a curving path into the city of Faesten, the Taura explained how the city was made. "We have lived inside this mountain since Ar-Rahman forged Amaris. Here we mine adiaperastos and akatalite, the only materials in our world that can cause harm to Sathariel and the Dark Forces. At the time of the Battle of Ulpan La Inyan, when she rose up against the people of Amaris, the Malevolents took control of one of our other mines, which contained akatalite."

A dark look passed across the Taura's face. "Now Sathariel has a metal that is indestructible and can cut through all other substances like a knife through soft cheese."

They were now down in the bowels of the city. The Taura paused outside a small house. Across the top of its doorway were dried herbs and flowers. The scent of lavender permeated the air. He knocked respectfully on the door, and a woman answered with rosy, red cheeks, like apples, and green eyes.

"Where's the patient?" she asked immediately. He eyes showed concern as she studied Afsana's pale face before Guilliaume swung himself off his horse and carefully carried Afsana's frail lifeless form in his arms.

"Bring her in, bring her in. We haven't got much time to lose," said the wisewoman as she ushered them into her home.

Guilliaume entered and laid Afsana down on a low couch that was in the corner of the room. Nadia and Yibinathi followed. The wisewoman smoothed down her apron and moved over to Afsana, checking her eyes and then her pulse as she placed a hand on her brow.

"We don't have much time at all. She must be a very strong young lady to have held on this long. My name is Sirona," she added almost as an afterthought as she began pulling jars from the shelves along the wall at lightning speed.

"Will she make it?" asked Nadia anxiously.

"I just don't know. But the fact that she is still with us is a good sign. And I'm not about to let one of the saviours of Amaris go without a fight."

Nadia gulped and stared into the flames of the fire in the grate. The room was full of the scent of spices and flowers. She watched as Sirona ran her finger along the shelves. She muttered to herself as she unscrewed tops, sniffed, and took a pinch here, and a spoonful there. All the ingredients were being put into a pestle. Every now and again she looked over at Afsana, who was drawing shallow and uneasy breaths.

Sirona licked her finger and paused thoughtfully. "We must have some of this." Then she pulled down another jar, which was full of dried leaves, and put it into the pestle. Grounding the mixture into a fine powder, she then gingerly stood on her tiptoes to reach a black box on the top shelf. Putting on a white glove, she carefully prized open the lid. With the utmost care, she took out a phial of liquid. Using absolute precision, she trickled three drops into the powder. It bubbled with an orange effervescent light, lighting up Sirona's face.

"Will you please hold the patient's shoulders," she asked, gesturing to Guilliaume. "Hold her as still as you can. This might not be pleasant for her. We have to purge her body of the poison, and I need to make sure we get it all out. We only have one chance at getting this right."

Taking a pipette, she gently opened Afsana's mouth and dripped three drops on her tongue. "Now brace her please," Sirona asked as she stepped back.

Afsana had been lying quite still. Her eyes suddenly flew open wide, and her body started to convulse. She gave a loud groan. Then her arms and legs went rigid. Afsana's back started to arch up from the couch, and she gave out an agonizing cry. Guilliaume was trying to stop Afsana's thrashing as she shuddered and convulsed. Nadia and Yibinathi watched as her veins started to glow with an orange light under her skin. They could see the liquid moving down the veins from her throat, her arms, and hands. It was pulsing through her veins.

"It's going to be alright, my dear, I promise." Sirona was watching anxiously. "This part will be over in a moment. It will pass." Afsana's eyes filled with tears and pain as her skin glowed. She squeezed her eyelids tight and gave a cry through gritted teeth.

"Nearly done," Sirona said, giving a reassuring smile. She took a white towel that had been sitting in a bowl of liquid by the couch. Afsana's body started to calm, and the tremors subsided. Her eyes fluttered shut and she appeared to fall into deep sleep. Sirona fashioned a press and put it onto the wound on Afsana's arm.

"Now, that's it. Let her sleep," Sirona cooed, patting Afsana's brow "She needs at least twelve hours to recover. Please leave her with me, and I will keep her safe and monitor her."

Nadia and Yibinathi nodded.

"I'm going to stay here with her," said Guilliaume to them both. "So when she comes round there will be a familiar face. You need to get to Brin."

Min-Ji looked up at the ceiling of the dirty stone-walled room. She couldn't understand why this was happening to her. She knew she had to get out, but she didn't know how. Thinking about all the different situations she'd faced while gaming, Min-Ji thought there must be some-thing she had done that would give her an idea. *I must have the knowledge and the intelligence to extricate myself from this mess,* she mused to herself as she looked around the carved stone walls of her prison.

Staring at the ceiling of the cell, she laughed ruefully. "I've swapped one prison for another!" But now it was like she was actually in a game not just playing it. "Okay," she said out loud, so she could focus on her words and the problem at hand. "What would you do, Min-Ji, if you were in the game? What strategy would you use? There must be something, there must be something I can use," she muttered as she looked around the room.

Min-Ji's concentration was shattered by a scraping sound as the door to the cell opened and Haigan entered.

"So Yasha, have you made up your mind what you're going to do?" he asked while sneering at Min-Ji. "Sathariel is offering you the world. Do you not see that she's offering you power? Isn't that what you've always wanted?"

"Do you think I would want to join her after what I've seen?" Min-Ji's asked as her eyes grew hard.

Haigan looked at her with a mixture of pity and contempt. "I think you underestimate Sathariel and what she can do to you. You underestimate how she can bend your will."

A strange distant look passed across his distorted face. "Sometimes, it's just easier to give in and say yes."

"Never." Min-Ji said and set her mouth in a firm line.

"So be it. When I return, you'll be able to tell Sathariel yourself. And we shall see what she does." Haigan shook his head. He turned and slammed the cell door.

Min-Ji let out a long sigh and stared at the slime dripping down the wall. She suddenly had a flash of inspiration. *A hummingbird came to get me,* she thought, *and a hummingbird was there distracting Sathariel. Did that mean a hummingbird could come and save me again? What if it was like when I was gaming? Could I call the hummingbird to me, in the same way I can call objects?*

She thought harder. *What if this world was just the same?* Min-Ji wondered if she could visualize and manifest the hummingbird in her life right then. She shifted uncomfortably. Maybe she needed to meditate. *Think positive thoughts. Stay present,* she said to herself.

Min-Ji closed her eyes and visualized the hummingbird in her head. She visualized every fleck of its iridescent plumage. Min-Ji visualized the hummingbird in front of her. She imagined it flying into the cell and being where she was.

Min-Ji spoke: "I'm here, I'm here. If you're going to come to me, if you're there, come to me, hear me. I don't know where I am or what's happening. But if you're here, come to me."

Min-Ji felt a tingling in her hands and a calmness came over her. She looked towards the light that was coming through the slit of a window in the cell door. She shut her eyes again. "Can you hear me hummingbird?"

The tingling was all over her body now. She felt a rush of

breeze. Opening her eyes, she saw the hummingbird right in front of her nose, beating its wings at lightning speed.

"Min-Ji! The Creator has heard you! We're here to get you out!"

Min-Ji would have done a victory dance if she hadn't been in shackles. "Yes! I did it!" She heard the bird's voice in her mind: "Trust you are going to be saved. Now listen very carefully, Yasha, and I will tell you why you are here."

$\mathcal{W}$ith the boys freed, Husam was ready to put a plan of escape into action. In hushed tones, he outlined his idea. They would convince Haigan to come into their cell and then imprison him. If they did this just before the guards changed shifts, they had a chance of getting to some of the higher unused corridors of the mine before their absence was noticed. Husam reasoned there must be a way out.

"Are you ready?" he asked them.

They all stared at him wide-eyed and frightened, but there was a steely determination there as well. Drawing themselves up to their full height, they all nodded. "Yes, we're ready."

The boys started yelling as Husam cowered in the corner of the cell while waiting for Haigan to come to see what the commotion was. The wooden panel opened abruptly, and the Legion leader pushed his pig-like face into the hole. "What's going on here?" he grunted, squinting his eyes this way and that. Husam was thrashing in the corner, moaning and screaming as he rolled around on the floor.

One of the boys pointed. "We can't control him. He seems to be having a fit! He's going to take us all down with him." He held up his shackled hands to demonstrate his point.

Haigan narrowed his eyes, harrumphed, and then turned the key in the lock on the door. He entered the cell, and his armoured bulk blocked the door frame. Husam doubled his efforts, rolling and moaning. "Help me! The pain, the pain!" He flailed his arms around.

Haigan grunted and stared at Husam who was rolling and writhing around on the floor. "When did this start?"

"When we came back from the mine floor, he just went into some kind of fit. Could it be contagious? You don't want everyone going down with it. I'm sure Sathariel won't take too kindly to us all being unable to work." One of the boys looked up at Haigan with a concerned look on his face. "Come closer; take a look. We're frightened of him." To prove the point the rest of the boys in the cell shuffled as far away from Husam as they could in their manacled feet.

Haigan moved into the cell and loomed over Husam's convulsing body. The moment he was clear of the door, two of the boys darted forward and looped their manacle chains around his legs. Haigan fell forward as they pulled his feet back. Another two swiftly shut the door to the cell. Haigan toppled to the floor. Husam rolled out the way and flicked his wrist, slicing through his chain using the akatalite. Tossing the stone to two of the boys, they sliced off their chains and deftly wound them around Haigan's wrists. Then they slapped the manacles on and tossed the akatalite back to Husam who re-fashioned his manacle into one flat piece of metal and shoved it over Haigan's mouth, muffling his grunts. He had been bound in a matter of moments.

"I'll take those thank you," said Husam, unclipping the keys from Haigan's belt. The guard stared at them angrily, his eyes full of rage. Husam started unclipping the keys, quickly handing them out to the group. "'Stay in pairs and unlock as many of the cells as you can. Once the doors are open, use the akatalite to split their shackles. Tell them to stay in groups of no more than two or three. That'll give them a chance to escape. Remember, keep going up. The more we split up, the more chance some of us have of getting out."

One of the boys, Kaushal, who seemed to be a leader,

nodded and asked: "Will you go a different way? So we can act as a diversion for you?"

"There's something I have to do," said Husam. "I need to try and find out where those boys are, the Malevolents…" he trailed off and shuddered.

Kaushal reached out a hand and put it over Husam's. "You're the Chosen. We will do everything we can to make sure you get out. You can trust us." Glancing down at the indignant Haigan, he reached for the Legion's belt, pulled a knife out, and handed it to Husam. "You might need this." He then turned to the rest of the boys. "Ok, let's go!"

Opening the cell door and slowly poking his head out, the boy looked left and then right. The corridor was empty. He turned and nodded, and the rest of them walked out into the corridor, keeping close to the wall. They disappeared into the shadows as Husam turned the other way and broke into a run. Trying to get his bearings, he was pretty certain that if he continued turning left, he would eventually come to the part of the mine floor where the boys who had met their terrible fate hours earlier were moved into another cavern. Husam knew he would be hundreds of feet up and hoped this would give him a good vantage point to see how he could get into the other part of the mine.

Before Sathariel had claimed this part of the mountains for herself, the Taura had mined it for hundreds of eons. And as they chewed through the cliff face pulling out akatalite, they had left behind walkways and tunnels. The stone itself was riddled with passageways. Some were dead ends. Others were shortcuts to other caverns. Coming to a fork in the dimly lit corridor, Husam paused, flicking his head one way and then the other. Suddenly he could hear shouts and commotion in the distance.

They must have found Haigan, Husam thought ruefully. Choosing the corridor on the left, he turned abruptly. The corridor had little light, and Husam figured it wasn't a path that was usually used. The rock glistened with moisture, and his bare feet slapped the cold stone as he ran. The corridor started to narrow, and he began to feel a sense of panic rising in his chest. The walls closed in as he continued forward. Soon he was not even able to raise his arms, and he had to crouch in the enclosed space. *I've made a mistake,* he thought. *This is a dead-end, and now I'm trapped.* Husam dropped to his knees as the corridor narrowed again and turned to the left. Knowing he couldn't go back, Husam decided he had to keep going forwards. Suddenly the corridor widened like a mouth, and he found himself standing in a small cave that looked out into the main cavern.

Gasping for breath, he stood with his hands on his hips. As his eyes adjusted to the light from the massive room, he could barely make out the other side of the cavern, pockmarked with caves just like the one he was standing in. To get a better view of the floor below Husam crawled along the path and gingerly stuck his head over the edge. He saw row upon row of boys. He gasped when he saw that their skin was deathly yellow pale, and they were staring blankly ahead, without a flicker of life.

Sathariel has built herself an undead army, he thought. *They were all boys once, living breathing people whose souls had been stolen from them by the Malevolents.*

Dressed in filthy rags, the undead army were ready for battle, brandishing an array of weapons ranging from swords and axes to catapults. Husam choked back tears. His heart was beating in his chest as he tried to stifle his feelings of anger, sadness, and horror. Taking a deep breath, he forced himself to focus. As he surveyed the cavern floor, he saw three Malevolents near one of the entrances to the main floor. They appeared to be at least ten feet tall, much larger than when Husam had seen them before. He reasoned they must have been growing from the power they were gaining from the souls of the boys.

One of the creatures glided towards the front of the rows of boys. It paused and its bony, scaly hands that had fingernails that looked more like claws slowly pushed back the hood of its cloak its skull-like face with pinpoints of flaming red where it's pupils should be. Husam turned away from the gruesome sight.

The Malevolents cloak fell to the floor, and it unfurled gigantic leathery wings. It raised an arm, and the boys all straightened to attention at once. The creature then swept its left arm out in an arc and the undead followed its outstretched hand. The Malevolent then gestured to three of the undead standing in front of it to come forward.

They moved jerkily like puppets, until they were standing in front of the best, staring vacantly into nothing. With what could be determined as a cruel smile, the creature raised its right hand, made a fist, and punched its own chest. The three undead lifted the swords in their hands and in unison plunged them into their breastbones, without flinching. The Malevolent let out a hoarse, triumphant, echoing laugh. "Sathariel's army is ready." it bellowed.

Husam pushed himself away from the cliff edge and gasped for breath. Now they knew what they were up against. And Husam knew he had to stop it.

13

Yibinathi and Nadia entered the throne room of the Taura. The vaulted ceiling was inlaid with gemstones, and the walls showed the marks of hundreds of pickaxes where the room had been created out of the rock itself. Their leader, Brin, was sitting on a throne hewn from twisted metal that had been spun into a fantastical geometric shape and inlaid with sparking rock and crystals. His beard was shot with spun gold, and a heavy chain of semi-precious stones glittered from his neck. At his side hung three swords.

Along each wall of the room, Taura stood at attention. Their armour shone in the light from the gigantic fire at one end of the chamber. Colourful flags hung from the ceiling. Brin cut a stern and commanding figure, but as the group approached him the Taura leader's face broke into a smile. He got up and gestured for them to move forward. "How is the other Yasha doing?" he asked.

Allurea moved forward and bowed. "Thank you for your help, Brin. Without Sirona's help Afsana almost certainly would have died."

He nodded in acknowledgement. Brin eyed Imamu and Etan suspiciously. "So, you need the Taura's help, yes? For many eons you have shunned us, calling us wealth obsessed and selfish because we have control of the mines of akatalite and adiaperastos."

"Brin," Etan said, "you have every right to feel ostracized. And yes, it's true that because of Sathariel, we have become too concerned with the protection of our own rather than of all of us. But now is the time to set these differences aside." He gestured to Yibinathi and Nadia and continued, "The Yasha have come and the Reckoning is upon us. We know the Chosen is in the Mine of the Malevolents."

Brin raised an eyebrow. "Is he? So the prophecy really is coming to pass," he said stroking his chin "Well, that really does put a different light on things." He got up and began to pace slowly. "So you not only need access to the mines, you will need the Sword of Rajwa."

Nadia coughed. "Your, err, majesty," she said, not quite sure how to address Brin. "My friend, Yibinathi, and I have the Fylakistone. If you can get us to the sword and help us rescue the Chosen, then our plan is to get rid of Sathariel for good."

Brin nodded. "Yes, and we can get our mine back," he said with glittering eyes. "But according to the prophecy, one of you is missing. There are supposed to be four Yasha."

"Yes," Yibinathi said, stepping forward. "Min-Ji was captured by Sathariel and we know she is in the mine with the Chosen."

"Hmm, well it seems like we could have a bit of a fight on our hands," said Brin as he smiled and rubbed his palms together. "As custodians of the impenetrable metals of Amaris, there is only one thing we like more than things that glitter. And THAT is getting down to it on the battlefield." Looking at Etan and Imamu, Brin narrowed his eyes and continued, "For the sake of Amaris, we will stand together with you. And we will offer the Hephaes to help you in your quest. I will accompany you to where they keep the Sword of Rajwa, and you can retrieve it with the Fylakistone. Then, we will help you free the Chosen and Min-Ji."

The leaders nodded their heads in agreement. Walking towards Brin, they extended their hands and put their fists together to seal their decision. Brin clapped his hands and smiled. "Now Yasha, let's go and get that sword."

<hr>

After what seemed like an eternity, they stopped. They had been walking through twisting tunnels, caves, and high suspended walkways for what seemed like hours. Nadia's eyes were sore from straining to see through the flickering torchlight. She felt a sinking feeling in her stomach. As the group shuffled out of the narrow corridor, they came into a cavern. In front of them was a wall of rock.

Brin turned to them. "The Hephaes already know you're here. They are at one with the mountain and will have felt your coming. If they want you to have the sword, they will give you access to it."

He asked the two Taura who had walked with them to step forward. Both were wearing huge drums which were secured by heavy straps. They began to beat a slow rhythm. "We are asking the Hephaes to come to us," said Brin in a low voice.

Nadia stared at the wall in front of her and swallowed a few times. How do you reason with a piece of rock? It wasn't like you could bargain with them. She shot a look at Yibinathi. He smiled and grabbed her hand. Nadia felt a rush of warmth and butterflies as he smiled to reassure her. The air was suddenly filled with a grinding sound, and the wall in front of them began to shift and move. As the rock rotated two giant figures appeared and stepped out of the wall in front of them.

"Who summons the Hephaes?" a voice boomed around the cavern.

Brin got down on one knee and gestured for Yibinathi and

Nadia to do the same. "It is Brin, leader of the Taura," he said with reverence. "I am joined by two of the Yasha."

Nadia frowned at Yibinathi. "How come we can understand them?"

"Maybe we can because we have touched the Fylakistone," he responded with a shrug. "Things work differently here."

The stone figure leant down and its face loomed above Yibinathi and Nadia. "You are here to retrieve the sword. The time of the Reckoning is upon us," the Hephaes said as it turned its gigantic stone head towards Brin. "Now is the time to put aside your distrust of the other people of Amaris, brother of the rock. We must all stand together against the common enemy. Set aside your differences when it comes to your beliefs." The figure gave a sound like a snort. "For they are all one and the same." Turning he gestured with a huge stone hand to the gaping hole in the rock from where he and his companion had stepped. "Come," it said, as the other figure started to move back into the rock mass and through the cavernous corridor. "Come, and we will take you to the sword."

Nadia and Yibinathi followed and found themselves entering a large room which was lit by glowing plants that were climbing the walls to a high ceiling where windows of light cut into the rock above. Nadia could see the stars receding with the dawn in the sky above them. As the prophecy had foretold, there was the Sword of Rajwa encased in stone that looked like it was made of moving water. In its hilt was a large hole where the Fylakistone should be.

The Hephaes pointed and said, "Yasha, take the Fylakistone together and place it in the sword."

"How do we do that?" asked Nadia. "It's rock!" She looked panicked. "And the Vanavashtha said they could only be joined where the sun hits the snow as it rises."

Yibinathi looked puzzled and first and then a smile crept across his face. "Brin," he said urgently, "where are we in the mountain?"

"Why, we're right at the top of the Mountains of Elphis," the Taura leader said, pointing upwards.

"That's it!' Yibinathi grinned with excitement. "The sun is going to hit the snow on the top of the mountains as it rises. How long till the sun comes up?'

Brin squinted. "Not long, see there," he said, pointing at a tiny shaft of light that was hitting the edge of the rock inside the windows.

"Nadia, we just have to wait and say the phrase at the right time." He pulled her forward, so they were standing in front of the pillar.

The Hephaes nodded. "Trust in the process," it said.

Nadia and Yibinathi stepped forward and got into position. They watched as the sunlight began to slowly flood through the ceiling. Then like a spotlight being switched on, the rays pierced down and hit the sword. As one, they took the stone and pushed it against the rock. Nothing happened.

"Why isn't it working?" Nadia asked. She was looking impatient and panicked at the same time.

"I think we need to say what the Vanavashtha told us," replied Yibinathi.

As one they recited: "*Bugan, Chabar Samani Aeternum.*"

The first time the rock wouldn't give. They repeated it and sweat formed on their brows with the effort. Pushing and gritting their teeth, they both tried again: "*Bugan, Chabar Samani Aeternum.*"

Nadia's eyes widened. She felt the stone give, like pushing a peg into a hole that didn't quite fit.

They recited the incantation a third time: "*Bugan, Chabar Samani Aeternum.*"

Suddenly the rock the sword was encased in gave way, and it was just as if they were plunging their hands into turbulent water. Together they guided the Fylakistone into the hilt of the sword. There was a click and the rock surrounding the stone turned into an exploding geyser, drenching them both. The force knocked them off their feet. Lying on the ground, the hilt of the sword in her hand, Nadia started to laugh. She rolled over and pushed her wet hair out of her eyes. Yibinathi, who was lying next to her, turned and his face split with a smile. They were aware of Brin whooping in the background as they raised their hands in a high five.

Yibinathi held onto Nadia's fingers and grinned. "Let's go and do some damage with this thing!"

On their return to Faesten, they discovered Afsana had woken up but was still very weak.

"Sirona wants to monitor her for a bit longer, but she is definitely much improved," said Guilliaume, who had been waiting for them, said with a smile. Yibinathi and Nadia glanced at each other with a look of relief. He continued: "She was most put out that she wouldn't be able to help rescue the Chosen and Min-Ji! She's definitely on the mend that's for certain."

The assembled Taura and the rest of the party gathered around the sword looking at it in awe. The sight of the Fylaki-stone reunited with the one thing on Amaris that could overcome Sathariel filled them with immense hope. Brin, after briefing some of his troops, had gathered together a group of his best fighters to accompany them on the rescue mission.

Now Yibinathi and Nadia, along with the divine interpreters, as well as Imamu and Guilliaume, were standing looking up at the sealed entrance that led from Faesten to the Mine of the Malevolents. Etan stood with the fifty Taura who were all armed with axes and swords and encased in Akatalite armor.

Brin turned to the group. "This gateway was sealed with Ruacha, which spread through every tunnel and walkway, so our part of the mountain was cut off from Sathariel's. The Hephaes can help us break through into the mine, and we can lift the binding on this section for a short while, which should give us just enough time to get in there and get the Chosen and Min-Ji out.' He gestured for the divine interpreters to come forward Allura, Allurea, can you help us?"

Allura walked up to the rock face, placed her hands on it, and closed her eyes. She took a few deep breaths and began to chant slowly over and over again: "*Patefio, transmineo perrumpo, perfringo.*" Her hands began to glow, and the light spread up through the rock face from her fingertips like rivulets of water. "This is a very old Ruacha binding that was used here Brin," she frowned. "We're not going to have much time to unpick it. I can loosen it enough for the Hephaes to break through, but you will have to hurry."

Allurea placed her hand on her sister's shoulder. "Let me help you loosen it, then you stay here, and I will go with the others to rescue the Chosen."

The two women held hands, and each placed a palm on the rockface, intensifying the spread of the glowing veins in the stone as they took up the chant together. As it widened across and up the rockface, Brin gestured for the Hephaes to move forward. Hulking towards the wall, they stood directly behind Allurea and Allura. The two women unlocked their hands and put both of their palms on the rock. They began to walk away from each other, their backs turned towards the edges of the wall. The Hephaes bowed their stone heads and lumbered towards the rock. Nadia frowned, as they looked like they were going to walk right into it. Then to her astonishment, they did exactly that. The Hephaes stretched out their arms and as if parting a curtain, walked into the rock, as their bodies pushed through it with a cacophonous grinding and popping sound. They passed into the rock face as if moving through water, and behind them was a hole where they had been. It was as if they were absorbing the rock itself into their bodies.

Brin waved the group forward as Allura and Allurea moved towards the edges of the tunnel that had been created by the Hephaes. The glow receded until it was lighting the tunnel being created by the two rock figures. Allura's face glistened with sweat. She kept her palms on the rock and gave a small gasp as Allurea took her hands off the stone. "You must make haste," she panted. The exertion of pulling on the Ruacha was tiring her. "This was designed not to be broken, I can only hold it for so long. May the Creator guide you with strength!"

Ahead, the Hephaes had come to a halt, and one turned its head to look at Brin, giving out a low rumble. The leader of the Taura nodded as he got the confirmation. "They've reached the other side of the rock and have reached the Malevolent mines. They won't make the final push through until we are there. One of the Hephaes can hold the exit point while we go and rescue the Chosen and Min-Ji."

The group entered the tunnel to stand in position behind the Hephaes.

Nadia turned to Yibinathi and said, "So this is it then. It's you and me. You got this?'

"*We've* got this." He smiled and caught her hand. Nadia smiled back as the Hephaes grinded out into the open of the mine on the other side.

***

*A*ll hell was breaking loose. As Husam ran back through the corridors into the main cells, he could hear shouts and screams. The boys had been good on their word, there was cell after empty cell with the doors wide open. They had obviously had a head start. Husam stopped to see a dead Legion guard lying on the floor. A chunk of metal hung out of his neck. The boys had obviously used their broken manacles as weapons. Husam careered along the corridor looking for a way out. He had to try and take advantage of the chaos. He knew if he could make it onto the mine floor, then he could find a way back out again. But he also knew they all had to get out before the Malevolents mobilized the undead army. They wouldn't have a hope of escaping if they had to stand against them.

Suddenly he heard shouting and the clash of metal. A Legion soldier burst around the ben in the tunnel, screaming. An axed was embedded in his armour. His face was contorted in pain as he tore past Husam not even paying him a second of attention. Husam had to press himself against the side of the wall to stay out of the way of the soldier as he careered past him.

There was a bellowing shout and within moments a Taura came barrelling down the corridor after the soldier shouting and waving an axe and hollering a battle cry. Husam pressed himself further into an alcove.

The Taura! They must have been able to break into the mine, Husam thought. Suddenly he was filled with hope. Maybe they could all get out after all. He headed back up the corridor and came to an area where six passageways met. In front of him Taura and Legion soldiers were fighting tooth and nail in close combat.

Husam knew if he could get to the other side of the passageway he could get down to the main floor of the mine. Their fighting was so intense he was able to stay pressed to the wall and manoeuvre around the melee.

He felt his way down the poorly lit corridor. Suddenly, Husam felt a blast of icy air, and a knot of fear clenched in his stomach. His breath hung in the air in front of him. Ahead of him was a Malevolent sniffing the air. Husam knew while they could smell humanity their eyesight was poor. The Malevolent sniffed again, inhaling and turned slowly. Husam shut his eyes tight, hoping the creature wouldn't sense him. Too late. With a swift movement it moved in front of him. The hairs on Husam's arms stood on end and it felt like thousands of insects was slowly crawling over his skin. The Malevolent leant in towards him, its eyes glowing dark red like coals of fire in the recesses of its hood.

"How would you like to enjoy the kiss of eternal life, boy?"

is hissed. When it opened its mouth and spoke the stench of death came from the bowels of its cloak.

Husam opened his eyes and was looking straight into the darkness of the creature's hood. It suddenly pulled back. "You!" came the rasping voice. "It's you. Where have you been hiding?"

Husam's brain was full of fog.

The Malevolent tilted its head that was hidden within the recesses of its cloak and rasped, "Sathariel has been looking for you. And yet it appears you have been here under our noses all the time." With another swift movement it moved forward and gripped Husam's hair, pulling his head back sharply. He gasped in pain as the creature slowly pushed his hair away from his face with its reptilian clawed fingers on his other hand. "The Chosen. What a prize Sathariel will give me when I bring you to her."

The Malevolent tilted its head the other way and Husam felt its cold glare sweeping over him even though he couldn't see its eyes. "Would you like to stand at the side of Sathariel? Would you like to rule over Amaris with infinite power? She can give you your heart's desire. She can make you… her king. You can rule at her side and enjoy the trappings of everything you could ever want." The Malevolent stood straight to its full height, filling the corridor.

Husam shook his head groggily. "I don't know . . ." he croaked and shook his head again. "No," he said more definitively. "You cannot tempt me," he shook the fog out of his head again. "You cannot convince me that Sathariel's way is the right way. Ruling with pain and horror, ruling with tyranny is not the way."

Husam shook his head again, feeling like it was becoming clearer.

"You have no power over me," he said with more strength in his voice. The Divine is a force that is far stronger than your evil. "The Divine gives us the power of free will. That is your weakness. You can't rule over Amaris by force."

Husam lifted his hand and pried the Malevolents hand from his face and took it in his wrist. "I will not rest until Sathariel has been *beaten!*" His knuckles were bleaching with the pain and determination of holding back the evil creature.

The Malevolent hissed and gave a low laugh. "I have seen into your mind. I know your fear. I know you have seen the power of the undead army." Husam winced as it rasped: "I know you fear you do not have what is necessary to save Amaris." The Malevolent gave a low cruel laugh. "Your doubts can be your downfall. Be aware that we will do everything to stop you from leaving these mines. Just because I can't take you by force doesn't mean that I can't imprison you."

The creature started to breathe slowly and the air in the corridor began to fill with acrid smoke. Husam felt like he was being suffocated. Tendrils of smoke began to wrap themselves around his body. As he struggled to remain conscious, he heard a bloodcurdling yell fill the air. Then a girl stormed into view down the corridor. She was whirling a sword around her head. Behind her was a boy about his age and what looked like Guilliaume, leader of the Elutheros, closely followed by Imamu, the leader of the Rehmat. Before he could even make any sense of what was happening, the girl ran at the back of the Malevolent waving the sword shouting and screaming. She jumped into the air and sliced the sword across the top of the Malevolents head and brought the blade down hard on its neck. The creature let out a bloodcurdling scream, and its cloak collapsed to the floor. A cloud of dark green ash dissipated into the atmosphere around them.

Panting and coughing, Nadia, who was holding the sword, stood upright and leant on it as she struggled for breath. She raised her head and gave a stunned Husam a crooked smile as she levelled her breathing. "You must be the Chosen," she said as she thrust out her other hand, which Husam took in bewilderment. "We've been looking for you." Nadia chuckled between grinning and coughing. "We better get you out of here."

14

*Y*ibinathi pushed forward and clapped Husam on the back "Good to meet you," he said. "I'm Yibinathi. Or, you might know us by—"

"You're the Yasha,' Husam interrupted with a look of shock. "This is really happening."

"Yep, it's really happening," said Nadia. "Err, not sure what we should call you? Saviour of the planet? The Big C? Or just the Chosen?"

Husam laughed. "Just call me Husam; it's easier. I'm not even sure how comfortable I feel with the Chosen at the moment."

"Right, Husam it is," said Nadia. She turned and noticed Guilliaume and Imamu were looking at Husam with reverence.

Husam blushed at their reaction. "Oh, stop that!" he chided with embarrassment. "First, thank you. But now, we have to get out." He looked over his shoulder. "I thought there were four of you. Where are the others?"

Yibinathi took the lead. "Ahh, Min-Ji and Afsana . . . about that. Well one of them nearly got killed by a giant snake. The other is in here—somewhere."

"Do you know about anybody being held in the cells who isn't being used to mine akatalite?" asked Nadia.

Husam shook his head. "Not that I know of. But there is an area of the cells I can take you to that is more heavily guarded, where the prisoners have less freedom than the rest of us who are working the mines. Sathariel uses it to hold prisoners she brings from the Dark Fortress who she usually plans to torture," he said with a grimace.

Nadia nodded, then took the sword she was holding and thrust it into Husam's hand. "This is yours. I'm pretty sure you're going to be needing it."

As Husam's skin touched the hilt of the sword the Fylaki-stone glowed, lighting up the dark corridor around them.

Nadia turned to Yibinathi and said in a low voice. "Well, if we needed any proof he's the Chosen, we got it right there." Husam gripped the hilt with both hands and thrust the sword into the air above his head and brandished a few practice strokes.

"I can't say I know what I'm doing," he said with a slight smile. "And I can't say I'm prepared, but I do know that we are about to change the future of Amaris."

Leading the way, he walked towards another tunnel. As they made their way down into the bowels of the mine, the walls changed. Soon they were bleeding slime, and the air was dank and wretched.

Nadia wrinkled up her nose. "Sathariel really doesn't want anyone to be found down here, does she?"

"You've got to be pretty special to be kept in this part of the mine," responded Husam.

Guilliaume stalked behind them, an arrow poised to fire from his bow. Suddenly there was a commotion. Bearing down on them were three Legion soldiers. Guilliaume shouted and started firing arrows as Imamu pulled a spear from her back. The three of them moved forward as one and locked arms with the Legion. It only took a few moments before the soldiers were on the floor. One was groaning in pain; the other had been slain.

Yibinathi started shouting. "Min-Ji can you hear us?"

A streak of light appeared and flew past the group, looping around, and stopped short in front of Husam.

"Hummingbird!" shouted Nadia triumphantly. "She must be here."

They renewed their efforts. The hummingbird zipped away in a blur and the group ran down the corridor following it.

"I'm here!" shouted a voice. They came to a cell. From within they could hear muffled cries.

"How are we going to get in?" asked an exasperated Yibinathi. "We have no key."

Guilliaume gestured to the sword. "On the contrary, I would say you have a pretty good one right there."

Husam smiled and signalled for the others to back up. "Stand clear of the door, Min-Ji," he ordered and took a huge swipe with the blade. It cut through the steel and thick wood like butter.

Guilliaume kicked the bottom part of the door down hard with his boot.

Min-Ji crawled out through the opening. Bewildered, and afraid, she peered at the group. "Are you the other ones like me? From Earth?" she asked.

"Yes, and we're here to get you out." Nadia held out her hand and Min-Ji grasped it. "We'll explain on the way."

They ran out onto the cavern floor where the Taura and the Legion were engaged in face-to-face combat. Meanwhile the boys who had escaped from the mines were brandishing whatever weapons they could find. The air was full of the bloodcurdling cries of the Taura as they faced down the enemy. Imamu rushed into the fray and joined Allurea who was now in the mine itself, using Ruacha to attack three circling Malevolents. The taste of blood and smell of sweat was in the air.

In a moment a hummingbird flashed in front of Nadia's

eyes. "We need to get you to the other side of the mine floor," it buzzed.

Guilliaume nodded. "Head towards Imamu and Allura; I'll cover you. Once we are close enough, they can protect you," he said as he pulled long daggers from each of his boots and handed them to Yibinathi and Min-Ji who each grasped hold of one. "Use these to protect yourselves," he advised.

The group formed a tight circle and started to move across the mine floor. Chaos reigned. Suddenly two Legion soldiers came running towards them, grunting and heaving, their faces twisted and bloody. Nadia screamed, and Yibinathi jumped forward and, imagining himself on his surfboard about to complete a jump on a wave, propelled himself into the air. He targeted the soldiers' throats and with one slash took them out in a gush of blood.

They edged ever closer to Allurea and Imamu. The leader of the Rehmat turned a gave a quick nod. Suddenly there was a rush of cold air; one of the Malevolents had spotted the group in the melee. Eyes on the prize, it swooped over, bringing with it the stench of death.

"Don't breathe in and don't look it in the face," shouted Husam. As the Malevolent veered towards them, Guilliaume unleashed arrow after arrow.

The creature hardly paused but let out a low hiss of anger, as though the arrows were merely an annoying distraction. As it neared and began to bear down on the group, Nadia turned towards some movement. Imamu had seen the danger. Giving a piercing call, within moments a flock of hawks materialized in the air around her. They began dive-bombing the Malevolent. As it was distracted, Husam gave a war cry and jumped up into the air with the Sword of Rajwa above his head. His sword met the creature with a loud clang, which climaxed in the Malevolents' howl of pain. Its body crumpled to the ground. The two other Malevolents howled in fury. The group were now right on top of Allurea and Imamu, who were covered in sweat with the exertion of using Ruacha.

"We have to get to my sister," gasped Allurea. "She is weak."

Guilliaume gave a low war cry. The fighting Taura broke from their battle for a moment, and switched formation, beginning to close ranks towards the group. Brin signalled to Guilliaume as they backed towards the mine entrance. Closing back on the passageway, the fighting was heated and intense.

"When I give the next war cry," shouted Guilliaume, "you run and bring as many of the boys as we can. The Taura will cover us."

Suddenly fifty Legion soldiers appeared on the other side of the mine floor. There were running towards them.

Guilliaume's voice filled the air and Nadia, Yibinathi, Husam, and Min-Ji turned as one and ran into the passageway. They didn't even turn around to see what was going on behind them. Hot on their heels was Imamu, glowing with the intensity of Ruacha.

As they rounded the corner the Hephaes were in sight, their gargantuan forms standing to attention. Around them were the littered bodies of Legion soldiers who had been crushed by all manner of boulders and rocks. Imamu brought up the rear as they ran into the passage through the mountain and towards the light at the other end.

As Nadia glanced over her shoulder, she saw Guilliaume and the Taura holding back the forces of the Legion and ushering as many boys as they could into the tunnel, which was filled with heat and light. As they burst out the other side, Allura was on her knees, drenched in sweat. Her hand was bleeding from the exertion of pushing it into the rock.

Suddenly the air was filled with a grinding sound.

"The tunnel is closing," shouted Imamu urgently. "We have to see who makes it."

Back in the mine the stone giants were moving through the rock as if it were liquid. The rock sealed back behind them as the tunnel closed. As the remaining Taura ran past their gigantic frames, the Legion soldiers and boys who had not made it all the way through were sucked into the waves of liquid rock, their bodies frozen forever in the tide as it turned to solid stone. Brin, the rest of the Taura and a stream of boys were coming out of the tunnel, coughing, and choking as the stone grinded in dust as it settled. They could hear screams echoing down the tunnel. Nadia screwed her eyes shut at the stomach-churning sound. Allurea staggered out of the opening and over to her sister, collapsing to her knees and gripping her sister's wrists. The Hephaes lumbered back through the void as the rock closed in like curtains behind them.

Allura let go of the rock face and laid on her back, breathing heavily. Brin, who was surrounded by a number of panting Taura, dusted himself off, and straightened his armour.

Eyes flashing with triumph he looked at the group, cleared his throat, and addressed the crowd. "Behold, the Chosen!" He raised his fist in the air and pointed it towards Husam.

All the Taura bent a knee, one by one. "The Chosen!" they shouted solemnly in unison.

Imamu and Guilliaume bowed deeply and then stood upright, raising their fists in salute. "The Chosen," they echoed. The rescued boys followed suit.

Allurea and Allura smiled and getting up from the ground gave a deep curtsey.

"The Chosen!" they shouted and the whole room broke out into cheers.

Brin let out a gigantic thundering laugh. "And now my friends, we return to Faesten, where we will feast and plan Sathariel's defeat!" The air erupted with cheers, and the crowd jumped in the air as one.

***

Azvameth hurried along the dimly lit passageways of the Dark Fortress. He looked more ancient than ever with his sunken eyes and sallow cheeks. To say Sathariel was on the warpath was an understatement. He could hear her screams and rage echoing down the hallways. The invasion of the mines had filled her with incandescent anger. Azvameth knew it was not going to be easy to convince her that they could overcome this setback.

The only silver lining of the situation was that their undead army was still ready to go into battle. But it was a huge blow; they had lost two of the Malevolents in the fight, and the Chosen and Min-Ji had escaped. It was no surprise that Sathariel wanted blood. Azvameth just had to make sure it wasn't his. Entering the throne room, he steeled himself for the onslaught.

Sathariel's voice was low and quiet with an edge of ice and steel. "How did this happen?" She was standing with her back to Azvameth and staring out the window. She held her black sceptre so tightly the veins in her knuckles were bulging.

"My queen, all is not lost." Azvameth dropped to his knees knowing that a sign of subjugation would bode well. "While we may have lost the Chosen," he continued, "the prophecy states he may not overcome you unless you can be imprisoned. How can he amass forces powerful enough to take you? Yes, he has his four companions. But the might of your army and the dark forces will surely overcome him." Azvameth's voice took on a tone of incredulity. "He is but a boy! You have seen the Yasha. They are barely grown. Mistress, if you amass the full might of your armies, if you call all evil creatures to your bidding, how can the Chosen stand a chance at defeating you?'"

Sathariel turned slowly. Anger was etched on her haughty features. She moved forward and stood towering over Azmaveth. With arms crossed she regarded him with a raised eyebrow. "You know as well as I do my fate is tied directly to the Chosen. The Yasha Prophecy states they must all be killed together otherwise I will die as well. The only way that can happen is if we capture them in the same place. My fate is directly tied to theirs. The only way we can overcome them now that we have the sword is by facing them head on in battle as it has been foretold in the Reckoning."

She stalked back across to the open window and clenched her fists. "I will not be imprisoned again." Narrowing her eyes Sathariel looked out at the barren landscape below her, a brooding expression on her face. "You have no idea or understanding of the pain and suffocation of being trapped in that stone for eons."

She turned back to Azvameth and snarled, "I will never allow that to happen to me again. Those who have risen against me will pay. The power of Ruach will overcome them. Now is the time for you to demonstrate your worth. We will summon every creature of the dark forces to stand at our side. We have an army of undead to stand down the hordes of those who believe they have the power to overthrow the might of Sathariel."

The queen thrust her hands into the air and brandished the warped metal sceptre. Her body began to writhe and twist as she pulled the power of Ruach towards her. "I summon you dark forces," she called, and a tornado began to gather around her. Azvameth had to lay down and push himself into the stone floor, grappling at the gaps between the flagstones with his fingernails so he didn't get blown away. But the force of the wind filling the chamber slammed his body back against the wall as if he were a dried-out twig.

"Malevolents, Obscura, and beasts of the night," screamed Sathariel, her voice screeching into the tornado. "All that which were once living and now cannot pass into the realm of the Creator," she called. Her features twisted as she pulled the all-encompassing power of the darkness towards her. "All manner of beings who once walked Amaris that now dwell in the twilight of death, COME TO ME!" Her high-pitched scream intertwined with the howling winds. The air was filled with a keening, haunting sound. She roared into the abyss of swirling darkness she had summoned around her. "Join me and fight with me to protect the world I have created FOR YOU!"

The air became thick, and the sound of whispers became deafening. "We are coming. We are coming. WE ARE COMING!"

<hr>

The city of Faesten was ringing with the sound of triumphant cheers. As the group made their way back towards the citadel, Taura lined the streets cheering and shouting. The bewildered boys who had been rescued from the mines looked around them wide-eyed. Babies were held aloft, and the Taura were thrusting tankards of beer into the air, cheering, and dancing jigs. Brin, his chest puffed up with pride, nodded and waved at the head of the procession as they made their way up to the heart of the city.

Turning to the crowd, he grinned and said, "This is the first of our victories. We still have a long way to go but we have won the first battle."

As they entered the citadel itself, Yibinathi, walking alongside Guilliaume said, "So now that we have the Chosen we have to raise the Caelum Bellator. Is that going to be hard?"

The Elutheran leader shrugged. "We have no knowledge if the Yasha Prophecy will definitely come to pass. My people have been guarding the Horn of Awaecnan for eons. And I will entrust it to you Yibinathi when the moment comes to awaken the Caelum Bellator. We have you, and we have the Chosen. We have to hope that you can break their slumber. This is ancient and powerful Ruacha we are dealing with."

Yibinathi nodded. "But we have the advantage that Sathariel doesn't know where they are."

<hr>

ow they had returned to Faesten, Nadia was enjoying the luxury of a change of clothes and a hot bath. As she shrugged on a fluffy robe and towel dried her wet hair, she still found it hard to believe everything that had happened to her in the last couple of days. She felt stronger than she ever had in her life. The bullies that had caused her so much anxiety and pain were a distant memory. She had never felt so free. And she had never felt less judged by those around her. Her life finally had a purpose. Nadia hoped she had what it would take to save these people. As she finished pulling on her fresh clothes, the door to the room opened and Afsana was standing there giving her a shy wave. Nadia rushed forward and enveloped her in a hug. "How are you? We were so worried. How are you feeling?"

Afsana smiled. "I'm feeling good. Tired but good."

"We thought we had lost you," Nadia said quietly.

"I thought I was lost as well," Afsana responded, tears pricking her eyes.

Nadia held her friend by the shoulders. "I have to thank you. You saved my life. It could have been me that got bitten. I owe you. I literally owe you my existence." She trailed off, not sure what else to say.

Afsana shook her head. "We're friends Nadia. I know we haven't known each other for long, but we're going through something no one else understands. It's something much bigger than both of us. Once, I was in a place where someone sacrificed themselves for me. And I vowed that if I could ever make that up I would."

They gave each other a hug. Nadia smiled and began to move around the room. "So now we have the Chosen and Min-Ji and all we have to do is wake the dragons and over-throw a psychotic who put Amaris on lockdown and kept its people prisoner for over a hundred years."

Afsana laughed and said, "No pressure!"

"Yep, no pressure there!" Nadia smiled at her friend. Continuing to get ready, she filled Afsana in on what the Chosen was like. "Husam, that's his real name, seems really nice. He's got a lot on his shoulders. Imagine knowing you're going to be like, the Saviour of the World. How do you cope with that?"

Afsana rolled her eyes. "I have no idea. But it's what I found myself asking when I looked in the mirror today. I realized we're in it as well!" They both fell about laughing and prepared to go to meet the others in the throne room.

The celebration was in full swing when they arrived. The air rang with the sound of laughter. Beer and wine were flowing, and music filled the air. The room was lit by the light of a thousand torches up in the rafters of the high ceiling. They waved at Yibinathi and Min-Ji who were seated at a table at the top of the room. Gilliaume beckoned for them to come over and take a seat. Nadia noticed the archer's gaze rested on Afsana just a moment longer. He smiled at them both and began to explain what lay ahead of them as they feasted on roast chicken. "The Caelum Bellator, the Koimeterion, are in their sleeping ground on the other side of the Mountains of Elphis. Imamu and Etan have already sent word and their troops are massing at Qualea where we will meet Nakoa." They all nodded as Guilliaume continued to outline the plan. "Brin is stockpiling armour of akatalite and weapons of adiaperastos for the troops. He and a small entourage of Taura will come to the Caelum Bellator with us, and the Hephaes will meet us with the rest of his army from Faesten.

Guilliaume looked over at Husam, who was deep in conversation with Allura and Allurea. He looked completely different now that he had cleaned up and changed out of the rags. His eyes were striking and commanding. And he held himself in a different way. "So that's our leader over there," Guilliaume said, nodding at Husam. "It's hard to believe."

"Why?" said Min-Ji, bristling visibly. "Because he doesn't look like he can do it? Because he looks different? Because he doesn't look a certain way? Because he doesn't fit the 'remit,'" she said, making air quotes to emphasize her point, "of what a 'leader'," she stressed the word with sarcasm, "is *supposed* to look like?"

Min-Ji pushed her roasted potatoes around her plate and then stabbed one forcefully with her fork before regarding it as she raised it to her mouth. "You know usually it's the ones that don't fit in, that don't *look* like they've got what it takes, who can make big things happen." She bit down forcefully on it and chewed as she stared at Guilliaume.

The archer looked slightly confused. Yibinathi, Afsana, and Nadia looked sideways at each other smiling.

Yibinathi clapped Min-Ji on the back in support. "You tell him!" He turned to Guilliaume. "I have to agree with her. From what I know of your world, you've all spent so long being frightened and wary of each other. You've isolated your-selves. He," he said pointing his knife in Husam's direction, "is going to give you the opportunity to overthrow Sathariel once and for all."

Nadia and Afsana nodded in agreement as Min-Ji blushed with pride.

Guilliaume smiled and nodded. "Yes, Yasha, wise words. I am standing behind the Chosen. It's time for us to take our home back."

15

*N*adia blinked sleep out of her eyes as she was being shaken by the shoulders. Allurea was leaning over her. "How are you feeling?" she asked.

"I'm feeling positive," replied Nadia. She gulped and tried to keep the quiver out of her voice. "I mean what could possibly go wrong?" She pulled herself out of bed as Allurea placed a pile of clothing on a chair next to the wash basin.

"I have every faith in your ability," said the divine interpreter. "There is a reason why you came here from your world. Each of you has an important part to play. Every one of you brings a different skill to enable the Yasha Prophecy to come true. You were not chosen by accident. Already you have seen how your individual skills and talents combine together." Allurea continued with confidence, "The Creator has a plan. Yes, we have our own free will, of course we do. But we have to believe that you have come together with the Chosen for a reason. To save our people." Allurea shook her head and continued, "The very reason Sathariel was able to take control of our world is because we were not united. Everyone went their own way. But when it comes down to it, we all essentially believe in the same power. The same mighty energy that runs through everything linking us all together as one. Yet we as people decided to twist and change that to our own ends." She sighed as she explained more. "Yes, my sister and my brother are the divine interpreters, who can only facilitate that power and interpret it in a way that can be understood by the needs of the people. And yet through their desire to interpret that power to their own ends, they have caused this terrible rift in our world."

Nadia nodded, thinking she was finally understanding the problem. Allurea had sat down and was smoothing down her dress as Nadia pulled on her clothes. After thinking for a moment Nadia said: "Faith is the power. It's the belief systems that cause the problem. And it's this fractured belief system, and our interpretation of it, that has allowed Sathariel to claim her foothold."

Allurea nodded and smiled. "Exactly, Yasha. This is why you are here. You see it." Smiling she rose and walked towards the door. I'll see you in the courtyard."

* * *

The citadel was alive with activity. As Nadia entered, she saw Husam talking with Afsana while Yibinathi and Guilliaume were joking together.

Brin cleared his throat to get the attention of the gathering. "We need to make it out of the south side of the mountains. Once we leave the safety of Faesten, we cannot guarantee that Sathariel's followers won't be watching us. Allura and Allurea will be using a shielding Goitera to try and hide our presence. My hope is we can make the journey down to the Caelum Bellator at the Koimeterion, their resting place," Brin continued.

Raising his hand, the Taura troops fell into formation, and the rest of them mounted their horses. Afsana was riding with Guilliaume on a horse named Akir after Kerren had been killed. She laid a hand on his neck before she mounted. "I'm sorry, Akir," she said, tears in her eyes. "She was a wonderful horse and companion. And thank you for carrying me when I was sick."

It was the first time she had been able to convey her sadness.

Guilliaume put his hand over Afsana's. "Akir thanks you for your kind words." They mounted and set off on their journey through the series of twisting mountain tunnels.

After a few hours of riding, the sun was coming up over the horizon. In the distance the snow-capped mountains were turning pink and then orange as the rays reflected off the white snow. As the mountain faces turned from crystalline white to dark rocky grey, Afsana's gaze travelled down the slopes to where grass and meadows began to fill up the vista. They were standing on the edge of a huge crater in the mountain range itself. It was a gigantic natural amphitheatre that had a shimmering azure blue lake in the middle of it.

"You're looking at the home of the Caelum Bellator, the Koimeterion," said Guilliaume in a low voice. "Thousands of years ago it was a huge volcano. It's said to have first come into existence by Eloah when he shaped Amaris. Our world was once nothing but roiling seas and darkness. Then with the light, he brought this volcano, Udbhava, into being. It's from this the land of Amaris was made. And with it triggered the creation of every being that walks our land."

"Yes, that has a few similarities with some of the theories on how Earth came about," Afsana mused. "There's also the school of thought that it was actually the power of nature and natural progression that was responsible. Personally, I like to think the big bang theory got the green light. That way, it's all about science and spirituality."

Guilliaume laughed. "Big bang theory? I like that!"

Afsana took a deep breath and sucked in the pure clean mountain air and took in the beauty before her. "I have to say it is pretty spectacular."

"The Udbhava crater is hundreds of miles across," replied Guilliaume. "The power of Ruacha runs strong here."

Imamu, who had been conferring with Brin at the head of the party, gave a low whistle to get everyone's attention. "We have a few hours to make it to the meeting place before the sun hits its zenith," she said. "As soon as we are in position, we can blow the Horn of Awaecnan and summon the Caelum Bellator. The hawks have reported so far the Goitera held in place, and now we are under the protection of the Shroud that covers the crater, which means Sathariel and her dark forces will not be able to see us." She turned her horse, pointed towards the lake, and proceeded down the scree covered slope to the meadow below them.

As they wound their way down the side of the mountain range, it became apparent there was a very definite path the horses were following. They delicately picked their way through the rubble and stones. As they began to near the valley floor, the sun rose higher into the sky. Afsana noticed indeterminable mounds of varying sizes around the valley itself. The mounds were at their smallest around twenty feet long and ten feet wide. They were covered in grass and flowers. As the sun caught the waving fronds of grass, some of them almost appeared to shift and move in the light. She breathed deeply, enjoying the tranquillity within the valley. The party itself was quiet apart from the low murmurings of conversation between Imamu and Brin and the jangle of the Taura's armour as they walked in double file ahead of them. The clip clopping of the horses' hooves on the scree was the only other sound apart from the occasional tweeting of birds.

As they neared the shoreline of the vast azure blue lake, the mounds became larger and more defined. Their shapes shifted and morphed with some appearing to have long protruding sections from the top and the bottom. At the edge of the lake were the largest mounds. There were three side by side, equally spaced out, that reached about thirty feet high.

"See that area of grey stones over there," gestured Imamu, "that's where we need to be as the sun hits its zenith."

Husam, Nadia, Afsana, Min-Ji, and Yibinathi all dismounted and followed her over to a plinth of grey rock that was at the water's edge. Embedded into it were numbers and letters written in a swirling script Afsana didn't understand. Peering over the edge into the water, she could see bottom of the lake dropped away sharply. She could make out huge fish swimming through the water.

Imamu had them sit in a circle and face the valley and mountains they had just descended. About fifty feet in front of them was a shard of metal rising out of the ground.

"When the sun hits that shard, you will see it forms a link of light to where we are standing," explained Imamu. "You must all stand on one of the letters, and Yibinathi will blow the horn. When I signal, hold hands and do not break the circle."

Guilliaume came forward, opened a velvet pouch, and pulled out the Horn of Awaecnan with great care. It was made from bone and had carvings on it similar to those on the stone on which they were standing. It had a silver and gold chord attached to it. He handed it to Yibinathi, who slung it across his body.

The group could feel the sunlight slowly creeping across the plinth. It was now hitting their backs as the sun between two of the mountain tops on the far side of the valley crater. They all looked at each other in expectant silence as their bodies began to warm up with the heat. Then Imamu gestured for Yibinathi to raise the horn to his lips in preparation to blow. In a moment, the sunlight, which had been creeping ever further forward, hit the plinth and crept up the metal shard ahead of them. The metal underneath their feet began to hum as it heated up. Looking around, it appeared they were all holding their breath. Imamu nodded, and Yibinathi blew into the horn as the sun touched the top of the shard.

The haunting sound echoed around the valley. As he blew

the second time, Imamu gestured for Husam to move into the centre of the circle. She stood aside and instructed everyone to hold hands.

Yibinathi dropped the horn, and as their hands touched, the metalwork started to glow with an intense blue light, and the heat began to increase. Like an echo that had been delayed, the sound of the horn filled the air. Yibinathi glanced down at the horn at his side. The stone plinth became encased in light. In a flash it travelled along the ground from where they were standing and hit the shard of metal, the light then shooting into the sky.

As Afsana looked up, it lit up a dome structure that was encasing the valley floor and reached way up into the sky above their heads. The blue light travelled through the shape like forks of lightning that set off a fine glowing rain, which began to descend on them. As it touched Afsans's skin it felt soft as a feather. The dome itself appeared to be disintegrating as the rivulets of light ran through its structure, raining down with a light fluttering sound like birds' wings. Within a matter of minutes, the rain of light had stopped. Afsana and the others looked at each other in the silence. Imamu was still standing in the middle of the circle, her eyes closed and head bowed.

"Did it work?" whispered Min-Ji. They were all looking around at each other and at the valley, not sure what to expect next.

It was quiet, apart from the birdsong. Then, slowly a breeze began to pick up. They felt the tendrils of it touching their faces. The lake behind them began to ripple, small waves lapping across its surface.

"Look!" gasped Nadia, pointing to mounds around the valley that were beginning to move. It was as if their surface had become liquid, and there were shapes moving underneath them, as if the grass and flowers were a blanket concealing something alive underneath the earth that wanted to get out. The earth itself appeared to be groaning as the mounds shifted and moved. Then directly ahead of them, there was a cacoph-onic cracking sound. The mound split in two and with an almighty roar the head of a dragon thrust up through the soil, which shimmered like water. The creature pulled itself upwards like it was swimming up through the ocean to come up for air. Its mighty head and shoulders came up as it clawed its way out of the mound. The dragon's skin glowed with flecks of gold and crimson as it pulled itself up and shook sleep from its majestic head. With eyes that glowed with fire, it reared up and unfurled its wings, shaking itself like a dog after going for a swim. The creature then sat up on its hind legs and appeared to give a huge yawn.

All around the valley, the scene was being repeated on every mound of earth. Dragons of varying sizes, and colours—green, blue, gold and silver—clawed their way out of their slumber. The group looked on in awe, and Imamu smiled with triumph.

Twenty dragons—in various states of awakening—were now preening themselves, and cleaning the dirt off their wings. Imamu gestured to Yibinathi, and he raised the horn to his lips and blew on it again. The dragons all swivelled their heads to look at him. And then as one, they gently laid themselves down with their chests low to the ground.

"Amazing!" he said as he turned to the group, stunned by what he'd just done.

On each of the dragon's chests was what looked like a papoose, which was attached with thick cord around their necks and bodies. The dragons, using their index claws, gently cut the chords so the papoose looking things slowly slid off their bodies to the ground with a soft thump. There was a rustling sound, and they gasped as a man's hand emerged grip-ping a knife. Slicing down the side of the structure, the dragon rider pulled it open and pulled himself out.

Absimil, the leader of the Caelum Bellator, ran his fingers through his hair and shook his head a couple of times before massaging his legs and arms for a moment. He then reached out his hands in front of him so he could gingerly stand up. The dragon rider was wearing clothing made of soft wool, and his hair was plaited back. He rubbed sleep from his eyes. Rising slowly, he blinked at the group in front of him. Around him dragon riders, men and women, were also slowly emerging from the cocoons as they stepped out into the sunlight. The giant golden dragon behind Absimil gave a soft croon as it gently pushed the leaders back with its nose.

"Woah there, Ayelet, I'm good," Absimil said with a laugh and swatted the dragon away playfully. Walking with a cautious gait, he came over to Imamu and the rest of the group. "It's been a long time," he said, thrusting out his hand to the Rehmat leader. She dropped to her knee and took his hand in hers with a firm shake.

She gestured for Yibinathi to come forward and hand the horn to Absimil. "I believe this is yours," she said with a smile. "You will know that if we have woken you, the time has come to fulfil the prophecy. The Chosen is with us," she said, gesturing to Husam, "and the Reckoning stands before us."

Absimil nodded. "I expect you have a lot to fill me in on. But first, we've got to get these dragons some food."

Taking the horn, he blew three short blasts. The dragons stretched out their wings and took to the air with slow lazy circles as they flew into a formation and headed out over the waters of the lake. They then took turns dive-bombing into its depths. Coming up moments later their jaws or claws were full of giant fish. The magnificent beasts then proceeded to fly over to the far shore and eat.

Absimil's dragon, Ayelet, who had already had his first round, returned to the lake for more. Coming up out of the water, he flew back over to where the dragon rider was standing and gently deposited a substantial mound of fish at Absimil's feet.

"Let's eat, and you can fill me in on everything," Absimil said to Imamu. "And I believe we are going to have to get out of our sleeping clothes and into something more appropriate for a battle!" He clapped the Rehmat leader on the back with a smile. "But first," he strode over to the circle they had been standing on and crouched down, "there's something I think you'll be needing."

Beckoning Husam over, he put a hand to his chest. "The Chosen, I would know you anywhere," he said looking into his golden eyes. "We have been keeping something safe for you." Gesturing for Husam to squat down with him, he took the horn and unclipped a gold disc from it. He then placed it in an indentation in the stone panel.

"Push your hand down here," Absimil said to Husam, indicating for him to press on the disc. Husam pushed hard, and with a click the stone gave way and fell inwards like a door.

Inside was a large circular box with a grid on top of small tiles that could be slid around in the framework. Each tile had a small image on it.

Husam frowned. "What does that mean?" he asked.

"It's a puzzle. Inside is the Shield of Aeras. If you can arrange the images in the right order, you can get the shield out."

Husam looked perplexed. "I don't know how to do it," he said.

Min-Ji stepped forward shyly. "Let me have a look. I have to do this kind of stuff in the games I play all the time. Maybe I can help."

She leant over. "What are these images of?" she asked.

Imamu and Guilliaume had joined them. "They're the pictorial signs we all use for the Divine, Eloah, what we call the higher power," said Imamu. She pointed. "Look, Absimil," she said, "there is the sign for Sraddha, your name for the Creator." Min-Ji thought for a second. "Okay," she said slowly as though deep in thought, "but, do you have any words that you all use that could mean come together."

"You mean like united?" asked Husam. "Yes, that's an

ancient word that comes from the old language that forms the root. We all use it *daeieis*."

"Can you organize the images so each image spells that out? So, for example, Imamu, the sign for the Divine would go first. Then you would have Ar-Rahman next. Does that make sense?"

Husam nodded and began to arrange the tiles on the grid. As he placed the last one in its hole, there was a loud clicking sound. The lid of the box swung open and inside was the shield. He leant down and pulled it out carefully.

Absimil smiled and placed the disc he had removed from the horn in the centre. Across the shield were images from the standards of the six clan people who dwelled on the earth of of Amaris—the Rehmat, the Elutheros, the Vanvasin, the Hayim, the Taura and the Caelum Bellator.

"Now, I think it's time for lunch," he said with a steely glint in his eye. "Then we will all be ready to win this war."

* * *

Yibinathi hooked his arms around the dragon rider's waist and hung on for dear life, as the wind rushed into his face. He screwed his face up tight as he gulped down a mixture of fear and excitement.

"I'm riding a dragon," he said to himself. Then shouting out loud, full of exhilaration the words whipped away by the wind, "I'm riding a dragon!" It was the most exhilarating, thrilling, and terrifying experience he had ever had. The slow sweep of the dragon's wings caused them to cut through the air, then there was a soft rushing sound as it rode the thermal air currents. Yibinathi opened one eye and looked down as the landscape fell away far below. He could make out tiny dwellings, rivers, and houses. Every now and then, they swept across herds of animals, which were startled by the dragons soaring above.

Only an hour before, he had watched in awe as the first

flight of dragons had taken off carrying Imamu, Brin, Guilliaume, and the dwarves that had accompanied them to wake the Caelum Bellator. The rest were carrying armour and weapons that had been taken out of the giant underground storage facility that had been kept hidden while the riders slept.

The dragons took off like a slingshot. You could see the amazing power rippling through their hind legs as they hunched down and prepared to power into the air. Then they unfurled their mighty wings and in a single power-driven movement left the ground.

The take off for Yibinathi had been the worst part. He felt his mouth drop into the pit of his stomach in a second. It was more intense, and nauseating, than when he was about to take a big wave. But once he was up in the air, he realized that flying a dragon was not that different than surfing. The riders were steering the dragons in the same way you guide a board through the currents and waves. He could feel their muscles rippling underneath his legs. It was that same intoxicating rush as he harnessed the power of a wave to ride it.

Their journey to the citadel of Qualea and the people of the Great Plains was only a short one, but it enabled Yibinathi to get a true idea of Amaris. He knew how much returning to Qualea since they had been banished would give Hayim and his people hope. When Sathariel had been overthrown, thought Yibinathi, feeling positive, they would be able to live there once again. He began to relax and take in the view. Next to him Afsana, Min-Ji and Nadia were riding on the dragons of the Caelum Bellator, and were just as in awe.

Nadia flashed a smile and gave him a wave, and he signalled back. It was one of the first times in a long time he had felt welcome—and part of something. In Sydney he was always the outsider. Here he was needed and wanted. Yibinathi didn't want that feeling to leave him.

Absimil turned and shouted over the wind in Yibinathi's ear, "You've got the knack for this. I think we can let you handle one of the smaller dragons. You have to learn to move with them and the current of the air. When they are fighting, it can get complex with the fire."

Yibinathi nodded. "It's a bit like surfing," he said, "something I do back home." The word *home* sounded foreign in his ears. For a fleeting moment he wondered how long he had been gone, or even if he would get back. Putting the thought to the back of his mind, he looked ahead and saw they were approaching a gigantic cliff that dropped thousands of feet. At the edge and down the side of the cliff hung structures arranged like gigantic limpets. They were intertwined with an intricate system of suspension bridges, stairs, and walkways.

To the left, was a vast area of tents. As they approached, Yibinathi could make out the different peoples of Amaris. The Taura, the Mountain People, were all arrayed in dark blue and grey and stood under banners of crossed pickaxes. The Hephaes rose out of the plain floor like monoliths, unmoving but observant. In soft shades of green were the tents of the Forest People, the Vanavasin. In the middle of the tents waved a banner of a tree fluttering in the breeze. Nestled close to their encampment were sapaksa, grazing on large bundles of leaves. Guilliaume's Free People, the Elutheros, stayed in dark red tents and had a bow and arrow on their banner. Rows of archers were taking part in target practice while others practiced hand-to-hand combat. The Rehmat, the Spirit People were also there, encamped in colours of yellow and orange. A banner emblazoned with flames signified their area in the gathering.

Absimil gave a low whistle. "By the light of Sraddha, the clans of Amaris haven't gathered together like this for 150 eons. Only the Chosen could have done this. It is sad that it takes a war against a common enemy to unite us. But if that is the case, then that can only be for the good of all."

Yibinathi nodded. Looking down he could see four Elutheros trying to catch their attention, waving gigantic panels above their heads to show where they could land.

Absimil raised the horn to his lips and blew a short staccato burst. The dragons began to fly in large circles as they prepared to land. They gracefully soared down and came to a halt.

As Yibinathi and the rest of them dismounted, Absolon was walking towards them, a kindly smile on his face. "Welcome! Welcome! The moment is nearing my friends!" he said as he gripped Absimil's arm. "At last! It's been a long time. You've missed the worst years thanks to your slumber, through no fault of your own!"

The dragon rider reached out and took Absolon's forearm in a firm grip.

"Where is Husam, where is the Chosen?" the divine interpreter asked. Husam stepped forward, and as he did so, Absolon bowed deeply. "A lot rests on your shoulders," he said. "But you have the full strength of Amaris behind you. You have given us the hope we need to overcome Sathariel and the dark forces. You have enabled us to put aside our differences in how we view the Creator and his plan for us. I thank you for that. We all do."

The party moved towards a tent where the other leaders were gathered. As they walked past the forest people, Yibinathi glimpsed a large tent full of gigantic dozing tigers.

"Etan and the Vanavasin ride the tigers as well as the sapaksa in battle," said Absimil, who had fallen into step alongside him. "See over there," he said, pointing, "the most magnificent of beasts."

Yibinathi glanced over to see a group of Rehmat carefully plaiting the manes of unicorns. Some of them were having their horns sharpened and tipped with vicious spikes.

"Imamu and her people ride unicorns. Don't be deceived by their gentle nature," said Absimil. "In battle they're ferocious and use their horns with great power."

"Does anyone ride anything that isn't spectacular?" asked Yibinathi.

"Well, the Hayim ride elephants and horses in battle,"

chuckled Absimil. "You will see, when we face down the dark forces, we need as many at our side as possible.'

Ahead of them was a white tent with a banner of each of the peoples of the Amaris fluttering on the top. Added to those he had already seen was a white flag with a dragon's head on it—the Caelum Bellator. They entered through the curtained entrance.

1 6

For the first time in an age the leaders of Amaris were assembled in the same room. There was a low murmuring in the room as the assembled group turned towards the entrance and watched Husam and the rest of the group enter.

Brin moved forward and raised his fist to his chest in a salute while Allura and Allurea gracefully nodded. Imamu moved forward with her fluid grace and placed her hands on Husam's shoulders and smiled warmly. Guilliaume nodded in greeting, as Etan and Nakoa also gave the breast salute.

As Nadia, Afsana Min-Ji, and Yibinathi surveyed the scene, they realized the true gravity of what lay ahead of them. Perched on the structured beams of the tent were two snow-white hawks, both observing with unblinking eyes.

Suddenly in a flash of light the hummingbirds Spark and Alar flew into the tent and buzzed up to Nadia and Afsana.

"You're back!" said Nadia smiling, and Afsana also grinned at the tiny birds excited turns in front of their faces.

"You made it!" buzzed Spark. "I never doubted you would be able to help us."

Absolon moved to the top of a table that had a large map with various coloured blocks on it. He raised his hand to bring the meeting to order. "Leaders of Amaris," he said, nodding at each of them, "the time of the Reckoning is upon us. The Yasha Prophecy, which we have held to us as a light and hope we will one day be free from the tyranny of Sathariel and the dark forces, is about to come to pass. As foretold, the Yasha came from another world to save ours. Sent to us by the Creator, they came to find the Chosen."

As he spoke, Absolon smiled at Nadia, Yibinathi, Min-Ji, and Afsana. "Sathariel used the dark forces to try and stop the prophecy from being fulfilled. We always knew there was the possibility she may overcome us. But here we stand on the dawning of a new era for Amaris. The hardest journey lies ahead for all of us. We know the great battle of the Reckoning is what stands between us and salvation." Looking at Guilliaume he continued, "The Elutheros have suffered terrible losses. Their own kind were turned into the Legion, Sathariel's army. They also lost their capital, Lutrectos, and saw the inhabitants lost as Revenir."

Turning to Imamu, Absolon said, "The Rehmat have seen their firstborn sons taken from them. Now fathers and mothers will have to face their own in an undead army." Imamu's eyes filled with tears, but she remained grim-faced and determined.

"We *will* stay strong against the enemy," continued Absolon, his voice remaining calm and steadfast. "The Creator has given us the strength to take on the might of the dark forces. Now is the time, people of Amaris, for us to set aside our differences. We need to unite against a common enemy, so we can be free once more. We know that the last words of the Yasha Prophecy are only that the Chosen will have the means to imprison Sathariel and release her grip for good. The rest is up to us to make this so. Now, let's put us in the best possible position to overcome Sathariel and end her reign of terror on our world."

"To the victory of Amaris!" shouted Brin, thrusting his fist into the air.

"To the victory of Amaris!" shouted Absimil. The rest of the room followed suit.

As their shouts died down, Absolon moved to the head of the table. "We are gathered at the edge of the Hesabu Plains. It is here Sathariel was released from the Fylakistone eons ago.

This is also where the power of Ruach and Ruacha was riven asunder." Pointing to their current place at the cliff overlooking the plains, he continued, "The hawk and hummingbird scouts have already revealed Sathariel is moving her troops from her base at Sclymgeour. The Obscura have been amassing, alongside the Legion and the undead army. We know she has lost two of the Malevolents, but she has others who have the power to guide the army. Also doing her bidding are any creature that she has overcome—some voluntarily, some under duress."

"How do we kill them?" demanded Brin, his eyes flashing.

"The undead can only be killed with weapons made from your adiaperastos," said Allurea quietly. "We don't know how many of them there are. Sathariel has been amassing her forces from the Elutheros and the Rehmat for eons. We will be facing a huge army."

"However, if they are not in akatalite armour, they are just as vulnerable to death as you or I."

Allura interjected, "The Malevolents can be killed by the Sword of Rajwa or dragon fire."

"So the odds are not in our favour?" asked Guilliaume.

"Theoretically, no," replied Absolon. "But the aim of our army is to get the Chosen close enough to Sathariel to trap her in the Fylakistone. This is the only way we can imprison her. It will be like cutting off the head of the snake."

Allurea continued, "If Sathariel is killed, then all of those who have been imprisoned by her, through her power, cannot be freed. They will die along with her. For as it says in the prophecy, before the end of evil, brother will fight brother, mother will fight son. Those who were once friends will have no choice than to face each other as sworn enemies."

Absolon spoke quietly. "Sadly, for the undead army, there is nothing we can do. Their souls are gone. But by the will of the Creator, my belief is they will be released back to the light with the imprisonment of Sathariel. Those who had no choice but to join her could be offered the chance of coming back to the light of the Creator; they must be given that opportunity once the battle is over. But for now we face them as the dark forces; we have to fight them as if they were our worst enemies."

"My feeling is we need to take as many out as we can by air," mused Absimil, staring intently at the map. "Etan, how many sapaksa do you have?"

The leader of the Vanavasin stepped forward. "There are two hundred with us. We can take Imamu's archers along with our own and then fly in low over the dark force troops. But we'll have to go in waves, so the dragons don't take us all out as well as Sathariel's army," he answered, tracing an arc and moving his green coloured blocks into place.

Absimil chuckled. "Yes, the power of dragon fire is an ace up our sleeve. But they will have to sweep first. Then you can go in as a second wave before we get to hand-to-hand fighting."

Brin climbed onto a stool that had been positioned at the side of the map so he could get a good vantage point. "With the Hephaes on the flanks we can use their catapults to flatten as many of the bastards as possible," he said while slowly scanning the battlefield map. "The only beings that have the power of overcoming them as far as I know are the Malevolents," Brin added as he swept his blocks into the fray. "They'll also be able to take out the undead army." Brin paused and looked kindly at the Rehmat leader. "Imamu, will your people be able to handle seeing your children again . . . like this?"

"They are no longer our children," Imamu said with a hardened look. "They're now but a husk doing Sathariel's bidding. But for every undead child we see in that army, we will offer a prayer to the Divine for their souls."

The group all nodded in agreement.

Absolon pointed towards the black blocks which represented Sathariel's army. "Sathariel will likely lead from the back," he said. "She will have Malevolents and Obscura along with Azvameth protecting her. She needs to be in the presence of the army as they are drawing their power from her Ruach. She is binding them together."

As he stroked his beard thoughtfully, Absolon turned to his sisters and continued, "I'll go ahead and seek out her position. She will be shielded. However, our brother's physicality grows weak as the power of Ruach eats away at his very soul. Our blood bond means as he embraces the darkness, he cannot hide the very essence of his being before it is overcome. I will infiltrate the dark force troops as the battle continues, and as soon as I have their whereabouts, I will communicate it to Allura and Allurea."

"We will provide the escort to get the Chosen as close to Satahriel as we can," said Imamu, placing a golden block representing Husam behind Etan's forces and surrounding it with a ring of several yellow ones.

"Allura and Allurea can you flank us so we can channel as much Ruacha as possible to provide a shield for the Chosen and the Yasha?" The two women nodded.

Guilliaume, the leader of the Elutheros, stepped forward and pulled his blocks onto the table in front of them. "The Hayim can join forces with us once we enter one-on-one combat," he said. "If they can go ahead with the horses, we will come in alongside the Taura. Imamu, I know many of your troops, as well as the Taura, have weapons made from akatalite and adiaperatos. We can move forward in a tier to take them out."

Nakoa, who was standing next to Guilliaume, nodded and added, "The key to this battle is using our wits against their numbers. And staying in the game long enough to give the Chosen enough time to get close to Sathariel. She, meanwhile, will be looking to take out the Chosen. So let us distract her might with the main battle, and you move closer to her location down the flank of the fighting."

Min-Ji raised her hand. "You need a decoy. You need her forces to think that the Chosen is somewhere he isn't. I'm prepared to do that."

"No!" shouted Nadia, Afsana, and Yibinathi in unison.

Min-Ji sighed. "It has to be done. If there's one thing I've learned while playing games, it's that you need to have more than one option when you're facing the enemy." Her face hardened as she continued, "When I was with Sathariel, she revealed to me her biggest flaw. She rules by fear, and she will judge your actions by her own methods. She is selfish and has no loyalty from anyone who follows her. They do so because they are morally corrupt or imprisoned or seeking some gain through the darkness. The concept of someone selflessly sacrificing themselves for the greater good of others is completely alien to her; she can't understand it." The leaders were listening to her intently as she continued, "Sathariel will assume if I'm the Chosen, you will do your utmost to protect me. It would never cross her mind that the Chosen would think to get close to her without the support and protection of the army. I also know that while Sathariel holds her forces together with Ruach, she can only see what they see. So if her army thinks they see the Chosen, she will believe it to be true. You need to get to her and get her sceptre which is what she used to embrace Ruach. Then you can use the Fylakistone."

Min-Ji added simply, "Make me the bait.'

Husam spoke. "Min-Ji, it's a selfless act. You know by doing this, you run the very real risk of dying?"

"I'm pretty good on a virtual battlefield. I think I can pull some nifty moves on a real one." Min-Ji smiled.

Absolon nodded. "Min-Ji, your bravery is commended. While we protect you with the troops, the Chosen will get closer to her with the Sword of Rajwa. Brin, you and the Taura will take care of taking out as many of the undead army as you can once we enter one-on-one combat."

The Taura leader nodded. He pushed his blue blocks onto the board.

"Turning to Husam and the Yasha, Absolon continued, "The task to imprison Sathariel is not going to be easy." Now, here is what you must do. To capture her in the Fylakistone, you must run her through with the Sword of Rajwa. But there is one very important part of the prophecy we don't know. To assure your victory and her imprisonment, you need to open the heavens."

Allura spoke. "The prophecy says: 'As Sathariel is held between life and death, the light of the heavens will be dimmed. The forces of light will be at the brink of destruction. But it is at the moment when all seems lost, that all is about to be won. Only the Chosen can bring the new dawning. The moment of purest clarity will signify when evil's reign will be finally overthrown. Balance must be brought between Ruach and Ruacha. The circle of life from this world and another will be completed. That which has corrupted will be torn asunder and held under. And the sun will rise on the new age of Amaris.'"

"What does that mean?" asked Afsana.

Absolon narrowed his eyes and explained, "We interpret it to mean that you, Yasha, and the Chosen, need to be present and be linked in a circle with Sathariel. Thus, the circle of light, dark, and another world are joined as one. But we do not know what that 'moment of clarity will be' or how you will open the heavens. This is where the prophecy stops short."

"Do you think it means a sacrifice?" asked Afsana.

"Possibly," mused Absolon. "We have prayed and asked for clarity from the Creator. But nothing."

"But Min-Ji won't be with us" said Nadia, "So how will this work if one of us is missing?"

"Once we have found Sathariel, we will get Min-Ji to you," Absolon said. "Absimil, we will need you to get her to the others."

The Dragon Rider nodded slowly and narrowed his eyes. "It's possible. Hard but possible."

Absolon continued, "Allurea, Allura, and I will deal with taking out Azvameth and holding back the dark forces so you can take on Sathariel. Once she is held between life and death, she will not be able to access Ruach. The fate of Amaris lies on your shoulders. We can only pray to the Creator and trust that we can fulfill everything that has been prophesied. The rest is up to you and fate."

Gesturing to his sisters and Absimil, Absolon moved to leave the tent and smiled at Husam, Yibinathi, Min-Ji, and Afsana. "The army will assemble at dawn. I will leave you to talk."

Kicking the edge of the rug, Nadia spoke first. "I know this doesn't seem easy. But I believe we are here together for a reason. I mean, if you had told me last week, I would be about to fight a battle to save a world from an evil overlord, I would have told you that you're stark raving mad." Speaking to Husam she said quietly, "I also look at Amaris and where we come from, Earth, and there are a lot of parallels. Your people have been divided by your beliefs, yet you all actually seem to follow the same thing. You all have faith, but you have let your own interpretation of it divide you. You are all alike, yet different, and you focus on your differences rather than what makes you have the same challenges as each other. By facing something terrible, you have been forced to come together and support each other."

Yibinathi, Min-Ji, and Afsana nodded in agreement as Nadia continued, "You have given them hope, Husam. We have given them hope they can come out of this. I know this seems like an impossible task, and there are so many things that could go wrong. But I believe we are here for a reason. And that reason is that we can't and won't fail."

Afsana agreed and continued, "We have all come together for good, and because of that we have a good shot at winning this." Looking around the circle she added, "You have your

Creator, your different versions of your Creator. But is he not the same?" So now you have to set aside your differences and focus on the real enemy, which isn't each other."

Yibinathi put a hand on Husam's shoulder. "How are you feeling about what you have to do?" he asked.

The boy with the golden eyes looked at the floor and suddenly appeared to be quite small. "Afraid," Husam said. "And also wishing I didn't have to carry this burden. I wish I didn't have to think about it. I wish someone would take it from me." He looked up at them. "I mean, why me? When growing up I always knew it might be me. My mother told me the story of the prophecy when I was a young boy, but I never thought I actually would be the Chosen. I'm not special."

Afsana touched his arm. "I think that's why you *are* the Chosen. You are normal. And because of that you can give people hope. There is nothing special about us either. Only that we all have our own challenges, and we all come from very different backgrounds from our own world. But now we are working together to make this happen."

Husam smiled shyly. "I don't think I could do it unless I had you all here," he said. "And we have to make this work. I don't want to see another soul get taken by Sathariel. I cannot see another animal or being on Amaris be imprisoned by the dark forces. We need to leave the darkness behind and join together. Put aside our differences and be united as one. Even if I have to sacrifice myself, it must happen."

"Agreed," said Min-Ji. "I found my purpose online in games. I was living in a fake world where I could hide from myself. Now I get a chance to make a difference for real. Now I get a chance to do it in reality."

Yibinathi gripped Husam's arm. "I was bullied and felt like an outsider for so long in our world. I thought I was different. And I don't want anyone to feel they have to be in fear every day they wake up. If we can make that stop here, then we have succeeded."

Nadia held out her hands and the group all stood in a

circular embrace. "Yibinathi, I was the same. I hated my life. I was frightened of myself, of stepping out and showing what I can do. If we do get home, I won't let anyone make me feel afraid again. I won't let anyone tell me I'm not good enough."

Afsana nodded. "My family and I lost everything and we had to leave our home. And it was because of war. Let's make sure no one on Amaris has to go through that. Let's end this war once and for all."

They all bowed their heads and tightly hugged each other in silence.

17

The sun crept slowly over the horizon. Its rays slowly reaching like tendrils across the plain. To the east, Sathariel and her forces were amassing. Their darkness was palpable in the early morning dusk. As the dawn broke, the Dark Fortress appeared on fire. Azvameth's Tower of Sclymgeour was jagged and stark in the barren landscape, where every living thing had ceased to breathe and exist. The two moons of Amaris could still be seen, the largest being blood red.

To the west, the Army of Light was getting into position. At the forefront of the troops, as tradition dictated, the Rehmat drummers, at the head of the battleline. Their drums were rolling with a thunderous steady beat. Behind them the Hayim whose horns would sound the advances. Armed with long knives and spears, their faces were painted with fearsome glowing designs. Their music would sound the march and channel the power of Ruacha through the Rehmat in battle. They would connect their troops with Ruacha and each other.

Behind them were row upon row of Elutheros, mounted and armed. The Vanvasin, shoulder to shoulder with the Taura, flanked the sides of the Army of Light. Archers from Elutheros were interspersed with Vanavasin, who were known for their superior bowmanship. On the cliff above the plain, the outline of Qualea rose behind them. The Caelum Bellator astride their dragons, waited patiently. The magnificent creature's were quiet but alert. Their breath steamed in the chill, as they rustled their wings in expectation. The Taura, wearing heavy armour made from adiaperastos, took up the left and right side of the flanks. Vanavasin, mounted on tigers, were interspersed throughout the central part of the army. Their tails were flicking expectantly. Their heads were encased in protective headpieces. The Rehmat, with their bows slung casually over their shoulders and riding high on the unicorns, made up a platoon. The Hephaes were in place with their slingshots armed and ready. Meanwhile the hawks circled above.

A low murmur was running through the ranks as the Army of Light felt the anticipation climbing as the sun slowly and inexorably rose further into the sky. A piercing horn blast silenced the low chatter as Husam, flanked by Nadia, Yibinathi, and Afsana, rode out to the front of the army. He stood surveying the peoples of Amaris, standing together as one for the first time in 150 eons.

Husam raised the Sword of Rajwa, the Fylakistone glinting in its hilt.

"Amaris," he shouted out across the army, who looked at him expectantly. "Today we are united with one goal. Today we are joined together as one to overcome the tyranny that has gripped our world for over an eon. For too long Sathariel has held you in her vice-like grip. For too long you have seen your loved ones suffer. You have lost those you hold most dear. You have seen your homes destroyed, and your future and hope snatched away from you."

The troops cheered as Husam nodded and surveyed them. "Now, today, the tribes of Amaris ride as one," he continued. "Against the common enemy that we *must* overcome. We have let our own definitions of belief shatter our unity. Today we ride as one with the power of the Creator. Today we set aside our differences in whom we worship. Let us put our own constructions aside and face our for under the one true force; the force of the Light."

The army let up another cry as Husam thrust his sword skyward. "We are *all* children of the Light," he shouted as the troops waved their weapons in agreement.

"Let us unify under this banner and fight that which has leveraged the split between us," Husam's voice grew to a roar as he continued, "Sathariel. Today, we will see Amaris freed, your people freed, and our new future born!"

The army erupted in whoops and cheers. The Vanvasin sounded their horns and beat their drums. As the Chosen, Nadia, Yibinathi, and Afsana turned around, the rising sun crept above the two mountains known as the Cradle of Atman. Its rays flooded the plain as the Army of Light chanted "For the Chosen, for Amaris" as it moved forward across the plain toward the dark forces.

---

*D*ressed in shimmering dark green metal, Sathariel with her now blood-red hair pulled back in intricate braids surveyed her own army. On a giant wolf, sceptre in hand, she looked out over the dark forces, which were marching inexorably closer to the Army of Light. At the head of her troops was her undead army, ready to be torn apart for her. They were loyal only because she stole their soul. She smiled to herself. These were now her children and would obey her every command. Joining them were the Legion, those that had bended to her will—some through choice, most through duress. But once they had all had a taste of the sweetness of Ruach, they were addicted.

Sathariel knew that when someone believed there was pleasure in stepping away from the Light, they were ready to abandon any need to experience goodness—especially once Ruach's perverse power had got its hooks into them.

Her eyes shone like fire as she watched the Malevolents glide silently ahead with the creatures of the night following them. Obscura, like giant leathery bats, their wings rasping in the cool air were flying overhead.

Behind her, the ghostly shapes of those who had been suffocated by the Fog of the Lost. Azvameth was riding alongside her, his forehead creased in concentration. He was channelling Ruach to hold back the undead until the moment the Light and dark forces met.

"I do not doubt we can win this war, Azvameth," sneered Sathariel. "Look at how our troops outnumber them. Even with their dragons," she laughed, "we still outnumber them. They will see that their pathetic attempt at *unity*," Sathariel spat out the word, "is a paltry effort in the face of my power."

Gesturing to her forces she turned to face him. "All these eons and the Creator has never once come to their aid. They have prayed to their God, and they have had no salvation. What sort of God sacrifices those that are supposed to be loved?"

Azvameth nodded and spoke with some effort as he continued to channel Ruach. "Of course, you are right. The Yasha Prophecy does not reveal the outcome of this battle. There is no doubt you have the ability to win and maintain your grip on Amaris."

Sathariel smiled cruelly. "They will see I have been toying with them. Every traitor who stood against me will lose their soul. My Malevolents will dine well when this day is over."

Raising her hand she banged her sceptre to the floor. The dark forces stopped their march as one. Ahead of them, the line of the Army of Light was coming into view.

"Now my children of the dark forces,' Sathariel said. "Now you will show me your loyalty. Sacrifice yourself for your queen!" she yelled. As she slammed her sceptre into the ground, a bolt of lightning shot up into the sky and lit up the plain as a roar went up from the army. With a loud horn blast, the Caelum Bellator took flight, and dark forces and Army of Light charged towards each other.

The dragons soared up into the air, and Nadia felt the wind push past her face as they were caught in the downdraft. Absolon had melted into the dawn light on his mission to get as close to Sathariel and his brother, Azvameth, as possible.

Glancing to the left of the army, Nadia could see Min-Ji in the centre, surrounded by a ring of steel. The divine interpreters had weaved a Ruacha binding on her and to everyone else she looked like the Chosen, even down to the sword she held in her hand. Nadia looked next to her and saw Husam on his horse, looking grim-faced. The smell of soot and fire caught Nadia's nostrils as the Caelum Bellator made their first sweep across the dark forces. The wind carried the tang of blood and bone as the dragons returned to the cliff, the second flight launching down across the fray.

Allura touched her arm. "We must start making our way towards Sathariel. I can conceal your presence for long enough for us to get through her troops. But once we get near her, she will sense the Ruacha and could see through your concealment."

Just then a piercing scream cut through the air. An Obscura had scored a hit and taken one of the dragons down. The majestic animal was plummeting towards the earth, its body overtaken by the wretched creatures.

"We must make haste," said Husam. He handed the shield to Yibinathi, who took up a position to protect their backs as they picked their way through the fighting.

The binding around Min-Ji prevented them from moving faster than a slow trot. It was a strange feeling, thought Nadia, to be moving through the edges of the battle, watching the fighting only feet away. She could almost reach out and touch them, but they had no idea of her presence. They moved past Taura, who were running full pelt into the army of the undead, swinging their swords of akatalite wildly round their heads and then shouting battle cries as they ran them through. Those lost souls crumpled to dust leaving their armour in a pile at the triumphant Taura's feet.

The Elutheros were wrestling with the Legion. Gripped in hand-to-hand combat, the smell of blood was thick in Nadia's nostrils. Meanwhile the Vanvasin on their tigers were taking on Sathariel's packs of giant wolves.

"How long do you think we'll be able to hold them off?" asked Afsana. She tried to keep the fear from her voice.

"Long enough for us to see Absolon's signal I hope," replied Allura, as she perspired from the effort of maintaining the binding.

An almighty roar split the air, and Afsana looked up. Her face crumpled as she saw another dragon plunge to the plain below in a ball of flame, writhing in the intensity of the Ruach blast that had hit it mid-air. An Obscura wheeled and swooped away hissing in victory.

In response to their hit, the Army of Light gave another blast on the horn and the unicorns surged forward full tilt into the fray. The Rehmat whooped war cries as the magnificent beasts, horns down, were ready for attack. As they flanked round, the thundering drums were drowned out by the noise of the unicorn's hooves as they descended at breakneck speed into the thick of the battle. Their snorts filled the air as they plunged their horns into the undead. They knew no fear with the most powerful female warriors astride their backs. Every misty form they encountered was skewered into nonexistence. The bodies evaporated into the air as they were hit by Ruacha and the unicorn's horns which were spiked with akatalite.

Roaring with rage, Sathariel thrust her sceptre skyward. Taking the sign to attack, the packs of wolves renewed their efforts and surged forward. Afsana could barely look as she watched the unicorns come under attack. Lunging and slicing with their jaws, the wolves began to overpower the magical beasts. The screams of mounted Rehmat and unicorns began to pierce the air.

Everywhere Nadia looked there was bloodshed. As their group made their way flanked by Allura and Allurea, it was becoming all too apparent the sheer number of the dark forces was overpowering the Army of Light. The two divine interpreters, their faces etched with the strain of maintaining their shield, continued to guide them at a slow trot. The fighting was fierce. The smell of brimstone, smoke, and death filled the air.

Grimacing, Nadia turned to the Chosen. "I don't think we have much time. There are so many of them. I just don't know if we can—"

"Don't even say it!" Husam said. His eyes were flashing with fury and fear "We *cannot* fail. Do not let your doubt get the better of you. This isn't over yet." His voice softened slightly. "We *can* do this. You can do this. It's when things appear at their darkest, you know you are about to come out the other side into light."

As if the Army of Light heard him, a shout of triumph rang across their forces. Four dragons swooped down low and fast and breathed fire over the frontlines of the undead army. Two Malevolents were caught in the flames and seared into oblivion.

All that was left of the undead army was the smouldering remains of their armour.

"Yes!" Nadia punched the air, and Afsana and Yibinathi let out a whoop. At that moment, a ball of light shot into the air and disappeared. It was long enough for Allurea and Allura to see where their brother Absolon was. The divine interpreters looked at each other and nodded.

Allura took on the pressure of maintaining the binding spell, so her sister could call to her brother with her mind's eye. She saw Sathariel encircled by a ring of Legion soldiers and flanked by the last Malevolent to her left and her brother Azvameth to her right.

The evil queen's face was twisted in intense concentration as she maintained her power over her undead soldiers. With all but one of the Malevolents now gone, the strain was beginning to show.

"That's where we have to go," Allura said, pointing towards a slightly raised area which was surrounded by the Legion.

As the battle raged in the sky above and the plain below, the group moved into the fray. They were so close to Sathariel, they could see her face. Suddenly Allurea held up her hand. "We must wait," she said in a low voice. "Absolon is going to confront our brother and try and reduce Sathariel's power."

Nadia watched as she saw the divine interpreter materialize next to Azvameth. The two sages faced each other.

"Brother, what have you become?" shouted Absolon above the noise of the battle. He stood opposite Azvameth, whose sunken face moved from an expression of surprise to incredulity to rage.

"You've been eaten up by Ruach; it's taken your soul. Do you not see what serving Sathariel and the darkness has done to you?"

Azvameth laughed. "Brother, my dear brother," he said sarcastically, sneering at Absolon. "Don't you know? Because she gives me something which the Creator never can and never will. Sathariel gives me complete power."

As Azvameth laughed, Absolon raised his hands. "Brother I cannot let you succeed today. That power, the darkness, is at the expense of life. At the expense of hope, love, and kindness. In the end it brings nothing but despair."

Creating a bowl of light between his palms he hurled it towards Azvameth. The sage responded and met Absolon's attack with a fireball of his own. This set off a spectacular and deadly display as the two divine interpreters attempted to overpower each other.

Absolon shouted, "Where is the grace and love in your

darkness? To feed the need of yourself, you have forfeited your soul. The instant gratification that her power gives you, see what it has done. It has eroded your humanity, your ability to love. The darkness has sucked away your life."

They continued to trade lightning blows as Azvameth screamed back, "Sathariel can make me as good as a god. Why should I answer to anyone? Is it not a prison to have to answer to a higher power? Are we not good enough to be gods?"

"We are not meant to like gods," shouted Absolon, and he landed a blow to Azvameth's side.

With a fiery crackle, Azvameth let out a groan and dropped to his knees.

As the lighting fight had raged between the two sages, Allurea and Allura had moved their group undetected through the fighting and were now just a few feet away from the warring brothers.

"Brother, you can still repent from this," pleaded Absolon. "The Divine will grant you forgiveness, if you ask. You can be forgiven. The slate will be wiped clean. Allura and Allurea, and I will forgive you. Whatever you have done, we still love you."

Azvameth stared up at his sibling, his eyes burning bright. "So you say you will forgive me? You say the Creator will forgive me?" he asked with a twisted snarl. "You believe this notion of love is the most important. That it can transcend anything. That the people of Amaris can put aside their differences and become one." Azvameth gave a low laugh. "How much faith you have in the fallible nature of our kind. Let me show what I think of your forgiveness, and family," he said as he spat on the ground.

In a split second his body twisted, and he shot a ball of light towards where Allurea and Allura were standing. As one the Chosen, Nadia, Afsana and Yibinathi bent over and shielded themselves as the two women stood in front of them to protect them. The light hit Allura hard in the chest. She screamed in pain. Allurea screamed in agony as she watched her sister collapse.

"Did you not think I knew they were there?" laughed Azvameth. Blood is thicker than water as they say. I knew of their presence as soon as they were within twenty feet of us.

Absolon looked at his sister's lifeless body as Allurea got on her knees and cradled Allura's head in her hands. Shouting in rage through her tears she screamed at Azvameth. "What have you done? You killed our sister." Turning to look at Absolon, the divine interpreters nodded at each other and raised their hands. A gigantic ball of light formed between them, and they hurled it at Azvameth. It all happened in a moment and before he even realized what they were doing he had been struck a fatal blow. Azvameth's body erupted into flames. With it, Sathariel's protective ring of steel forces. The Legion and Malevolent evaporated into dust. Allurea and Absolon raised their hands again and drew a circle of blue fire which rose twenty feet into the air.

Within the circle, Nadia, Afsana, Yibinathi, and Guilli-aume, were still present, along with Sathariel and the Chosen. The queen, who had been focusing her attention on keeping her dark forces on the attack, turned as Azvameth was incinerated.

Yibinathi looked at the scene and grabbed Husam's arm. "Give me the shield. I have an idea."

Sathariel, who was reeling from the loss of Azvameth, doubled over as she took on the strain of channelling Ruach to control her army.

"So that is how this will be," she hissed with hatred in her eyes as she realized she was trapped.

Taking in the Chosen, the evil queen felt a stab of uncertainty. Then she recovered in a moment. "Now you will witness the true power of Ruach. See how I will make your Divine," she spat, "and the Army of Light bow before me."

Raising her sceptre, the sky filled with rolling storm clouds. Green lightning forked up into the heavens and then split into two bolts, creating a dark void. From within, a dark ocean was broiling and raging. Rising up through the depths, as if crawling into the storm clouds above the plain, a Leviathan erupted, roaring and thrashing as if pulled out of its sleeping place. The beast was bigger than any dragon. It had two serpent heads, which were thrashing and hissing as they breathed down a blue fire across the Army of Light. As the Caelum Bellator tried to attack, the Leviathan blasted them, turning the majestic creatures to ash.

"Watch as I wipe your army out forever, Chosen!" Sathariel's eyes burned as she stared at Husam.

"We have to get the sceptre from her," shouted Nadia to Yibinathi and Afsana. "All she's going to be worried about is the Fylakistone and being imprisoned. Husam can keep her attention." She looked at the archer, who was firing arrows into the fray around them. "Guilliaume, can you cover us?" Nadia asked.

He nodded and they pulled back as Husam moved towards Sathariel.

The Chosen was circling the queen, crouching low as he tried to get closer to her. "You know the prophecy says you will not win. Your reign of Amaris is over," taunted Husam.

"Does it?" spat Sathariel. "Because everything has to come to pass for that to happen. You know there is another way." she wheedled. "You could rule with me, at my side. Why would you not take that over being supplicant to the Divine. If you were truly loved, would you have been imprisoned by me? Would your people have been persecuted? What kind of god is that? You have suffered so much, and the Divine allowed it to happen."

Husam frowned. "But what freedom do I have with the power of darkness? Surely you are as much a slave as you say I am?"

As he spoke, Nadia, Afsana, and Yibinathi moved stealthily towards Sathariel.

"You have the freedom to be what you want, to control who you want. To make others bend to your will. There is so much more enjoyment in that," laughed Sathariel.

"But why would I want someone to obey me?" asked Husam. "You don't have any power at all. You don't have anyone following you of their free will. That is why you will never truly have power. And all those that you believe worship you, there is no love there. There is no loyalty. What good is that?"

Sathariel's eyes flashed with anger. In that second her guard dropped, and Nadia saw their chance as her grip of her sceptre loosened. "NOW!" Nadia shouted as she rushed forward. As Guilliaume let fly arrows as a diversion into the blue fire, Nadia lunged forward and in a rugby style tackle move slid along the floor to knock the sceptre.

Meanwhile, Yibinathi, who had been brandishing the shield to protect them, suddenly had a thought. He jumped into the air, wedging his feet into the edges of the metal. Using the shield like a surfboard he spun into an arc, imagining he was hitting a wave. At the same time Nadia pushed the sceptre up into the air, Yibinathi twisted in a mid-air pivot, grabbed it, and threw it to Afsana. Brandishing the knife of akatalite she had been given by Brin, Afsana smashed it into the orb and split the diadem in two.

Sathariel screamed in anger as she lost her grip on her army. "Did you think that was my only source of my power? You cannot stop the Leviathan, even if you stop me. And you have not stopped me yet. And you can't," she thundered triumphantly. "You are not united. One of you is missing!'

"Min-Ji!" Nadia gasped. They couldn't complete the circle.

The queen's face was alight with triumph as she spat out the words in a roar. "I will *destroy* you. You cannot fulfil the prophecy!"

Husam looked at Yibinathi, Nadia, and Afsana, desperation etched on his face. Sathariel was right. Allurea and Absolon looked at each other. They opened their hands wide and thrust the power of Ruacha up into the sky, splitting the dark clouds as if parting the ocean. A thunderous roar filled the air and heat and light pierced through the roiling sky. It was Absimil, flying in low on Ayelet, through the pathway that had been created by the divine interpreters.

Absolon and Allurea were brought to their knees as they embraced the immense amount of Ruacha needed to create the space. The Leviathan was shrieking in fury. It couldn't get to the dragon through the barrier. Min-Ji was perched on the dragons back and ready to jump.

Ayelet plunged down skimming over the top of the battle wrecking a trail of havoc with his fiery breath.

Absolon and Allurea shouted out. "Jump now!" It was a hundred-foot drop to the ground.

Yibinathi waved and slung the shield up into the air. "Grab it! Trust me!" As Min-Ji jumped the shield spun up, and she managed to catch hold of the metal. It rotated her around acting like a parachute.

"What?!" shouted Nadia incredulously.

Yibinathi grinned in a moment of respite. "It's like it's made of air!"

As Min-Ji thudded to the ground completing the circle Husam looked directly into Sathariel's confused and angry face.

"Ah Sathariel, but we have fulfilled the prophecy," shouted the Chosen in triumph as he ran forward and thrust the Sword of Rajwa into her body.

Sathariel doubled over, hissing, and spitting in pain. Husam grabbed hold of Nadia's hand and Yibinathi, Min-Ji, and Afsana rushed forward to complete the circle. Blood was running from the corners of Sathariel's mouth as she gasped for breath. A rushing sound began to fill the air, and the Fylak-istone started to pulse and change colour. Sathariel's lifeforce was being drained from her body and sucked into the heart of the stone.

Through ragged breaths she rasped, "The Darkness will stop you. The Leviathan was brought from the depths. All the time that exists, the dark forces will continue to march. I am just a vessel for the true Darkness. I am not the source of Ruach. That which goes before me is the source."

As her body began to wither, she stared into the Chosen's eyes. Full of loathing she gasped, "This. Is. Not. The. End." Sathariel's body shrunk back on itself, turning from a skeleton into dust in mere moments. There was a sigh as the sword clattered to the ground, intertwined with the remnants of what Sathariel had worn in the battle.

18

The Chosen grasped the sword and thrust it into the sky. "Divine hear us! Send us your light." The Sword of Rajwa glowed in his hands. A huge thunderclap split the storm in the heavens and the sun burst through the clouds. The Leviathan paused in its attack.

Nadia looked up and shielded her face. Squinting through the brilliance, she could make out the outline of a winged shaped soaring through the sun.

"The Kaluduta!" gasped Guilliaume. "The right hand of Eloah." The winged beings soared through the stormy skies. The Leviathan cowered and thrashed as several Kaluduta surrounded it, pushing its mass toward the broiling depths of the split in the sky from which it had come. Flying in circles around the beast, they created ropes of light that held it tighter and tighter as they moved it into the roiling depths of the darkness.

Other Kaluduta swooped down low over the dark forces, waterfalls of light emanating from the tips of their wings. As it hit the undead army, they disappeared.

The solitary Malevolent that had escaped the blast of Azvameth's destruction, seeing the winged beings, fled into the skies towards the dark void.

The Kaluduta on the edge of the hole riven in the sky, in a catapult movement swung the Leviathan back into the Darkness. Then in a blaze of blinding intensity, the rift disappeared.

As Nadia and the rest of the group gazed up in awe, the Kaluduta swept down across the troops. Their waterfalls of light cascaded down and healed those who were injured on the battlefield.

Husam stared in wonder as one of the beings came down and hovered before him.

"You are the Chosen," it said. Its voice sounded like the tinkling of bells and was no more than a whisper but imbued with the power of the loudest thunderclap. "The Creator honours you and your companions for saving Amaris. Lead the people and be set free."

The winged creature seemed to shift and shimmer at the edges. Husam found it hard to gaze at it as it hovered before him and spoke. "Let it be known the Creator will bless the land which was taken away and heal that which was broken." With that, the Kaluduta ascended into the skies, and in a blaze of light, rose into the heavens from where they had come.

"Look!" Afsana said, pointing as the Kaluduta, their wings shining in a blaze of glory, disappeared into the clouds.

On his knees, Husam wiped his hair away from his face. His other hand was trembling as he still clutched the Sword of Rajwa.

"You did it!" Nadia shouted while jumping up and down. "You freed Amaris!" Nadia slapped Husam on the back, as she grinned from ear to ear.

Across the battlefield those who had been imprisoned as Legion soldiers by Sathariel were staggering to their feet as if waking from a long sleep. Bleary eyed they looked around as if not knowing when they were. They were restored.

Absimil swooped down on his dragon and landed next to Husam. Jumping off he got down on one knee. "You have delivered us from the evil of Sathariel," he said, looking up at the Chosen. "We are forever indebted to you. Permit me to take the stone and place it where Sathariel can never endanger the lives of the people of our world again."

Husam nodded and pulled the stone from the hilt of the sword and handed it to the dragon rider.

Imamu came striding towards them across the battlefield. She stretched out her hand and put it on Husam's shoulder. "Our people are free," she said. Her eyes shone with tears of joy. "I will journey with Absimil to place the Fylakistone where it cannot be found. Brin will help create an impenetrable stone fortress to make sure there is no way she can escape."

Min-Ji stepped forward. "Husam, let me help design a trap and barricade system to make sure it will be almost impossible to retrieve the stone."

Husam smiled and nodded. Gripping her arm he said, "Are you sure you want to stay and do that?"

Min-Ji nodded. "I always knew all those hours of playing games would come in handy. Now I can actually use some of those skills I learned to help create something real."

"Does that mean you're planning to stay?" asked Afsana.

"Only for a little while," said Min-Ji. "Absolon told me that once we have the stone fully secured, I can return home. Being here has made me see there's more to life than sitting in front of a computer screen. I didn't realize people would value me for who I really was, who I really am. But here I've discovered I have just as good a purpose in the real world. And I can be me. Now I can use what I'm good at for the good of others. And hey, I always wanted to design my own game, and that's kind of what I'm doing, right?" She laughed.

Afsana grinned. "Well, when you do make it back, you had better not be a stranger."

Min-Ji shook her head. "Who knows how we'll find each other on Earth? That's going to be another adventure, right?" She gave Afsana a hug and Yibinathi, Nadia, and Husam completed the circle.

*B*ack at the encampment there was pandemonium. Everywhere the people of Amaris were celebrating Sathariel's demise. Taura and Vanavasin dancing and cheering. The Elutheros slapping the backs of the Rehmat and hugging each other. Their differences and fear set aside with the victory they had secured. The Yasha, the Chosen, along with Guilliaume, Absolon and Allura made their way to the Strategy tent where the other leaders were waiting.

Walking towards the same spot where they had mapped out their battle so many hours previously, they were cheered from left and right walking through the pavilions.

Shouts of "the Chosen," and "the Yasha" filled the air. Renewed positivity and possibility charged the atmosphere.

Nakoa, Etan, and Brin got to their feet as the others entered the tent. Absolon smiled. "Today is the new dawning. The Reckoning is over. The Yasha Prophecy has been fulfilled. Husam has united the people of Amaris, and we are free from the tyranny of Sathariel."

His face darkened and he turned to his sister Allurea. "My biggest regret is we had to sacrifice lives in the process. But from that loss I know we will see wonderful things grow and renew. And I know my sister would never have wanted it any other way. We will make sure her sacrifice was not in vain." Everyone took a moment to remember those that had been lost in the battle.

Absolon turned to Husam. "Now your destiny is to keep Amaris united," he said solemnly.

Brin stepped forward. "Know this," he said. "The Taura will follow you . . . we will follow you to the ends of the earth."

Etan stepped forward and put his fist to his chest. "We also will follow you. You have our loyalty."

Guilliaume joined them. "You have freed us and our people. We have suffered greatly under Sathariel. But now our

Lutrectos will finally be restored to us. Our lands will be our own. We swear fealty to you, the Chosen."

Nakoa nodded. "You also have our full support in the unification of the Hayim. For too long we have been forced to ride alone, forced to wander the plains without our home. Now we can finally return to our citadel and make it ours again."

Husam nodded at each of the leaders in turn. "Thank you for your honesty and your fealty. I have much to learn, and I have much to learn from you. I think we can all agree that what we must do is put aside our differences. Working together is what brought us together. It is what gave us the power to overcome the evil that infiltrated our lands. It is what enabled us to become the strength that was needed to overcome Sathariel. I propose from this moment on we forget our differences, and let us unify together and trust that the Creator is the overarching truth for us all."

The leaders thrust their arms into the air as a sign of agreement. Absolon spoke. "The force of Ruach and the damage it did to the lands around Sathariel's Dark Fortress are already receding. The balance is being restored, and the natural beauty of Amaris is beginning to return. Ruacha is breathing life into that which was made barren. You will be able to have those as yours."

Allurea stepped forward. "May I propose that my sister's Tower of Sikali becomes a monument to those that died and sacrificed themselves in the battle."

Husam nodded. "You have my word," he said.

"We will stand behind these decisions," said Brin with sincerity. "We will work together with you and the divine interpreters to keep peace and harmony across our lands. And now," he said turning to the rest of them, "all that is left to do is celebrate!" His voice rose to a roar. "To our freedom."

The rest of them cheered. "Our freedom! To the freedom of Amaris!"

our days had passed since the great battle of the Reckoning. With Husam now installed as the leader of Amaris, everyone had returned to their own lands. After an emotional farewell, Yibinathi, Nadia, and Afsana were back at the Tower of Sikuli with Absolon. Min-Ji was still working on the fortress that would guard the stone to keep Sathariel imprisoned.

As they crossed the meadow to the Thura Gate that led between their world and Amaris, Nadia felt scared. What was going to happen to her when she got back? Would her life be the same? How long would she have been gone? Would she remember anything? Glancing over at the other two she could see that they were clearly anxious too. "Absolon, are things going to be different?" Nadia asked, her face full of worry.

Putting his arm around her shoulders the divine interpreter furrowed his brow. "What you have done here has made you different people. So yes, your actions and the events that have unfolded due to you being here have changed the future of our world forever." He stopped and looked at them all. "It was your destiny to come here and save us. Everything unfolded the way it did because of who you are. You had to find your own bravery and strength. You had to trust and overcome your own battles within you to help us overcome our battle."

Absolon smiled and then continued, "Nothing happens in the universe without having an effect on somebody else. Just one tiny action can trigger a million others that can change the face of a world in a way we cannot even comprehend. I cannot tell you what your world will be like when you get back. I do not know the answer to that question. But I do believe that what you've done here has caused you to grow and change and that will affect your lives when you return."

"I wonder, will I go back to the refugee camp," asked Afsana.

"Yeah, and will I have to deal with being made to feel like an outsider all the time?" said Yibinathi. "Or now that I've ridden a dragon, maybe I'm going to be a way better surfer."

"Now," Absolon said, speaking to all of them, "you have the ability to believe in yourself," said Absolon, "and that will make you even stronger and better at anything you do."

Nadia said: "All I know is that when things get really rough, I'll have this to hold onto. I'll know that whatever people say to me, I'll know I saved a world. And there's not much that can top that."

They had now arrived at the Thura Gate. It loomed before them so unassuming, and yet they knew for the second time their lives were about to change once again.

Looking at Absolon, Afsana asked the question all of them wanted to know the answer to. "Can we come back? If you needed us or even if we needed you?"

Absolon gestured to the marks on their hands. "You are forever connected not only to each other but to this world. Now you know what those marks mean. There are many prophecies in our world, many which were hidden by Sathariel when she took over. Allurea and I intend to retrieve those prophecies from Lutrectos, now that it's been restored to the Elutheros."

He smiled. "It may very well be this won't be the last time you come to our world."

They all nodded.

"Now," said Absolon, taking a step back and gesturing for them to enter the stone. "Are you ready?"

"Yes," they said in unison.

Nadia, Yibinathi, and Afsana looked around before entering the stone. They all knew that despite travelling together, there would be a moment when the Thura Gate would push them to their own destination back on Earth.

They entered it just like before. Inside the intricate designs were still there. The cracks and crevices were splintering through the stone. Nadia, Yibinathi, and Afsana held hands and looked at each other with trepidation.

"This is it," said Nadia. "Maybe now our adventure is really just beginning."

<hr>

Somersaulting through the depths of the void, the Malevolent's body spun over and over. Circle after circle. The pressure was bone breaking. But it knew it would only last for so long. In the darkness the voice filled the Malevolent's mind. "My servant, you failed me."

Its body was wracked with pain, as the dark forces held it in its vice-like grip. Shuddering in pain it rasped, "Show mercy to me. Let me prove to you we can still overcome the Creator."

The voice answered. "Prove to me your worth. And this time, I do not expect you to fail."

THE END

GLOSSARY OF NAMES

Amaris (Hebrew) – given by God

The Divine Interpreters
Absolon (Hebrew) – father of peace
Azvameth (Hebrew) – strong death
Allura (French) – entice or attract
Allurea (French) – entice or attract

Religions of Amaris
Dragon Riders/The Caelum Bellator – Sraddha (Sanskrit) - faith
Forest People/The Vanavasin – El Shaddai (Hebrew) - another aspect of God
Free People/The Elutheros – Eloah (Hebrew) - God
Mountain People/The Taura – Ar-Rahman (Arabic) - the merciful
Plains People/The Hayim – Imani Mungu (Swahili) - faith in God
Spirit People/The Rehmat – The Divine (taken from Greek) - referencing God

The Yasha – The Four

Afsana (Urdu/Persian) – story
Min-Ji (Korean) – clever and quick-witted
Nadia (multiple languages) – hope
Yibinathi (Zulu) – be with us

The Chosen

Husam (Arabic) – sword of justice/ injustice

The Dark Forces

Sathariel (Hebrew) – 17th fallen angel, 'side of God'/conceal-
ment of God
Haigan (Gaelic) – young
Legion (Latin) – troops
Leviathan (Hebrew) - a great sea monster
Malevolents (Latin) – ill-disposed and spiteful
Obscura (Latin) – shadowy/indistinct winged creatures
Revenir (French) – the Undying – back from the dead

The Forces of Light

Hephaes, the stone giants (Greek) – Hephaestus, God of Stone
Kaluduta, Winged Army of (Arabic) – sent from God
Sapaksa (Sanskrit) - having wings
Vanavastha (Sanskrit) –one who gives up earthly life/roots

Places, Portals and Sacred Objects

Adiaperastos – material that can harm Sathariel and lost souls
Aeras, Shield of (Greek) – air
Akatalite (derived from the stone Atlantislite; healing and
stabilising)– indestructible armour and metal
Apokalupsis, chest of (Greek) – apocalypse
Awaecnan, Horn of (Old English) – awakening
Durara Gate (Spanish) – it will last
Fylakistone (Greek) – prison
Goitera (Sanskrit) – good enchantment

Obscura (Latin) – shadowy, indistinct
Ophis, Pits of (Greek) – serpent
Rajwa, Sword of (Arabic Islamic) – hope
Ruach (Hebrew/ Greek) – bad power
Ruacha (Hebrew/ Greek) – good power
Sambandh (Hindi/ Sanskrit) - relationship/ bound or fastened together
Sunasi, Tower of (Indian) – seeking wisdom
Sclymgeour, Tower of (Scottish) – fighter
Sikali Tower of (Sanskrit) – knowledge and fairness
Sikuli, Tower of (Sanskrit) – teacher, confidence
Thura Gate (Sanskrit) – brave

Historical Amaris
Battle of Ulpan La Inyan (Hebrew) – religion
King Ciman (Hindi) – curious
Queen Atropos (Greek) – stop at nothing

The Clans of Amaris
The Forest People, The Vanvasin
Etan, their leader (Hebrew) – firm, enduring
Myrkvior, the capital (Germanic) – in the trees
Vanavasin (Sanskrit) – forest dweller
The Mountain People, The Taura
Brin, their leader (Welsh/ Celtic) – hill
Faesten, the capital (Old English) – fasten
Taura (Indic) – mischievous/ haughty
Elphis, Mountains of (Greek) – hope
The Spirit People, The Rehmat
Imamu, their leader (Swahili) – spiritual leader
Salama, the capital (Swahili) – safe
Rehmat (Urdu) – blessings
The Plains People, The Hayim
Nakoa, their leader (Hawaiian) – defender/ warrior
Qualea, the capital (Arabic) – fortress
Hayim (Arabic) – wanderer

The Clans of Amaris

The Dragon Riders, The Caelum Bellator

Absimil, their leader (Hebrew) – my father is peace

Paracletes, the capital (Hebrew) – breath of spirit

Caelum Bellator (Latin) - sky warrior

Koimeterion, (Greek) - sleeping place

Ayelet, a dragon (Hebrew) – new dawn

The Free People, The Elutheros

Guilliaume, their leader (French) – gilded helmet

Heliopolis, the capital (Latin/ Greek) - city of light

Elutheros (Greek, adapted) – free-born not bound

ABOUT THE AUTHOR

Zoe Nauman is a journalist, copywriter, editor, and speaker, who has worked with some of the world's most well-known brands and publications for over twenty years. She's an expert storyteller with a penchant for helping brands find their unique voice. And as a journalist, she's interviewed some of the world's biggest celebrities, including Angelina Jolie, Nicole Kidman, and Lionel Richie.

A globetrotter by heart, Zoe moved from the UK to Sydney, Australia, in 2008, living there for seven years while traveling to some of the most beautiful parts of Asia — including her beloved Bali. She's now in westside LA and spends her days writing, corralling her three chihuahuas (Chica, Poco, and Enzo), eating blue cheese stuffed olives, and running on the beach.

CPSIA information can be obtained
at www.ICGtesting.com
Printed in the USA
LVHW011753120422
715979LV00005B/578